TRESPASSERS

JON ATHAN

Copyright © 2019 Jon Athan
All Rights Reserved.

This is a work of fiction. Names, characters, businesses, places, events and incidents are either the products of the author's imagination or used in a fictitious manner. Any resemblance to actual persons, living or dead, or actual events is purely coincidental.

For more information on this book or the author, please visit www.jon-athan.com. General inquiries are welcome.

Facebook:
https://www.facebook.com/AuthorJonAthan
Twitter: @Jonny_Athan
Email: info@jon-athan.com

Book cover by Sean Lowery:
http://indieauthordesign.com/

Title page font (Horroroid) by Daniel Zadorzny:
http://iconian.com/commercial.html

ISBN: 9781693587832

Thank you for the support!

First Edition

WARNING

This book contains scenes of intense violence and some disturbing themes. Some parts of this book may be considered violent, cruel, disturbing, or unusual. This book is *not* intended for those easily offended or appalled. Please enjoy at your own discretion.

Table of Contents

Chapter One 1
Chapter Two 17
Chapter Three 25
Chapter Four 33
Chapter Five 47
Chapter Six 55
Chapter Seven 59
Chapter Eight 67
Chapter Nine 75
Chapter Ten 87
Chapter Eleven 93
Chapter Twelve 107
Chapter Thirteen 115
Chapter Fourteen 129
Chapter Fifteen 145
Chapter Sixteen 159
Chapter Seventeen 167
Chapter Eighteen 177

Chapter One

Broken Homes

Crystal Cox lay on her bed and stared at the ceiling. Black bags and webs of wrinkles surrounded her dim blue eyes. The ceiling was a few feet above her, but her eyes were looking at something miles away. A drop of blood from her left nostril rolled down her cheek, leaving a thick red streak on her pale skin. The blood reached her ear, then it dripped from her earlobe and landed on her dirty blonde hair—*plop, plop, plop!* It soaked into her pillowcase, too. The tips of her fingers were burnt, pink and purple and swollen and peeling. She tasted traces of blood each time she licked her chapped, cracking lips.

A glass crack pipe, stained black from its bowl to its mouthpiece, sat on her nightstand. Her drug of choice: *crack cocaine.* She was itching for another gram, another rock, one last hit before she called it a day. But she was out of money. She wore a McDonald's uniform. She worked as a cashier and made eight dollars and sixty cents an hour. A rock of crack cocaine demanded twenty-five dollars from most dealers in the area. She couldn't support her drug habit with that meager salary. She squeezed out four hits per rock—five, occasionally. And those hits amounted to less than an hour of euphoria.

She grew dependent—*addicted*. One hit led to another and so on and so forth. In her ideal world, she would have been smoking twelve rocks a day, maintaining a perpetual high during her conscious free time. She never considered the possibility of overdosing. She didn't fear death. Death didn't even cross her mind as she chased the little white mouse through her euphoric dreams.

On her bed, as still as a corpse, she brainstormed some money-making ideas. Prostitution came first. She didn't own anything valuable to resell, but she owned her body. *People love sex as much as they love drugs,* she thought, *how much am I worth?* She groaned and shook her head. She had a boyfriend and he would have killed her if he caught her selling herself on the streets. So, she figured she didn't *really* own herself.

She considered theft, but her options were limited. She couldn't steal from her family because they were broke. They owned a high-definition television but they didn't pay for cable, they owned an old computer but they weren't connected to the internet, and they owned cell phones but they didn't have service. Her father, John Cox, earned a decent living by working at a construction site, but he spent his money on their rent, alcohol for himself, and drugs for his addicted wife.

"Rock bottom," she whispered. "What am I supposed to do? Beg? Stand outside the grocery store and–and *beg?* I can't..."

Oro City was a small city in Nevada, about twenty-five miles away from Las Vegas. The population barely cracked ten thousand. But small cities had the loudest voices, and social media amplified those voices. Rumors spread as soon as they were created, like a baby born with HIV. She feared someone would take her picture and post it online to humiliate her. *I'd be a joke,* she thought, *a bigger joke than I am now.*

A tear rolled down the left side of her face, parallel to the blood leaking from her nose. She felt her skin crawling, as if all of her nerves were tingling. She shivered and let out a shaky sigh.

"Did you take my beer outta the fridge?" John asked.

Crystal lifted her head from the pillow. She found her father standing in the doorway. John was a big, burly man with broad shoulders and a firm beer belly. His brown hair was thinning and his beard was patchy. He stood there in the doorway to his nineteen-year-old daughter's room, wearing a tattered wifebeater, soiled boxers, and slippers.

John said, "I was savin' that beer for after work. I said, '*don't touch it, it ain't for you.*' Didn't I say that?"

"I didn't touch your damn beer. Get out of my room."

"Your room? Girl, you don't even pay rent here. So, you better watch your mouth when you talk to me, you ungrateful cunt."

Crystal sat up and asked, "What do you want me to pay for, huh? For this little bed–"

She stopped as her blood dripped onto her lips. She swiped at her face, then she looked at her hand. The confused look in her eyes said something along the lines of: *when did I start bleeding?*

John said, "You don't pay rent 'cause you're busy getting high like your *stupid* mother. You're fuckin' useless, Crystal! You! Are! *Useless!* Now give me my goddamn beer or pay me!"

"Pay you for what?!"

"For my beer!"

"I didn't take it!"

John marched into the room. He approached her old, rickety dresser. He threw her wrinkled clothes aside and searched for any cash or something to sell. He found crumbs from old drugs—marijuana, meth, crack—stuck in the cracks of the wood.

Crystal shouted, "Don't touch my stuff, asshole!"

"It ain't your shit! I paid for *everything* in this goddamn room! I pay for everything in this goddamn house!"

"*I* pay for my stuff. *I* have a job."

"Bullshit. You barely make enough to pay for your crack, you little whore. Then you go out and give the rest to that dumb boy out there. You ain't foolin' me."

As he looked through her drawers, Crystal grabbed the back of John's shirt and pulled back with all of her weight. John lost his footing. He stumbled towards the door. Crystal rammed him with her shoulder, launching him into the hall. She slammed the door, then she turned the lock. She stomped and screamed at the door, then she jumped back on her bed face-first.

"Leave me alone," she whispered as the doorknob rattled.

"Open this door!" John barked. "Don't play this game with me, girl! Open up!"

"Leave me alone, leave me alone, leave me alone," Crystal repeated as she curled into the fetal position.

A dead silence followed. She didn't hear the kids or the cars outside. She didn't hear her father in the hall or her brother in his bedroom. For the first time in years, her home was quiet and calm.

The door burst open with a loud *crashing* sound. The doorknob fell apart, screws bouncing on the floor while the knob spun in place. John tackled his way into the room, red-faced and blood boiling.

He shouted, "Who the hell do you think you are?!"

"Get out! Jeez! I don't have your–"

John slapped her. Her head fell over the edge of the bed, hair dangling a few inches above the floor. In a daze, she sat up and sniffled. Before she could compose herself, John struck her with a backhanded slap. She fell over the *other* edge of the bed. Blood oozed out of her gums and cascaded over her teeth. She mumbled incoherently as she sat up again.

John jabbed his index finger at her and said, "Don't *ever* touch me again, you cunt. Now, where's your money? If you ain't got none, I'm takin' your drugs. One or the other, you choose, girl."

Crystal coughed, then she spat a blob of blood on her bed. A piece of a chipped tooth rode the gooey blood like a surfer riding a wave. She huffed and rolled her eyes. She stared vacantly at the broken door. She listened to her father pull out all of the drawers on her dresser and nightstands, feverishly searching for something—*anything.* Like his daughter, he suffered from addiction. The alcohol withdrawal took a toll on him.

Crystal didn't care about it. It wasn't the first time he struck her—and it wasn't the worst. There was a squiggly vertical scar on the left side of her forehead, from her hairline to her eyebrow. She covered it with her hair so people would stop asking about it. When she was sixteen, before she ever experimented with drugs, her drunk father threw a glass beer bottle at her. The 'funny' thing was: he did it for the same reason. He believed she stole some of his beer.

She trembled, she gritted her teeth, and she clenched her fists. She couldn't tame her anger anymore. She jumped up to her feet behind her father. She kicked him between his legs. Her shin hit everything from his scrotum to his anus. John crouched, put his knees together, and held his hands over his crotch. He waddled until he faced his daughter. Lungs full of air, he tried to speak, but he could only croak and groan. A vein, which appeared to be slithering under his skin, bulged from his forehead.

Crystal said, "I didn't take your beer, asshole."

"I–I... I ca–ca..."

Crystal kicked him again. The tip of her shoe slid past his hands and landed on his scrotum. He gasped and fell back. He crashed into the dresser, then he fell to his side. He screamed and squirmed on the floor. The pain was debilitating.

"I hate you so much," Crystal said as she stared at him with disgust written on her face. On the verge of crying, voice breaking, she said, "I'm leaving this... this... this shithole. *This hellhole!* This fucking terrible place! I'm leaving and I'm never coming back! Fuck you and your beer!"

She ran across the hall and went into her brother's room. Cody Cox sat at his desk, headphones blaring as he tried to ignore the chaos. The lamp on his desk illuminated his math homework and his chewed pencil. He was a fifteen-year-old high school student, and he was struggling to keep up with his classmates. He thought about dropping out every day and following in his sister's footsteps. He wasn't a drug addict, though. He smoked marijuana, but he wanted to quit.

He took his headphones off and slicked his hair back as he glanced over at his door. His eyes widened as he spotted the smeared blood on Crystal's face. He was younger than his sister, but he acted like an overprotective older brother. His instincts told him to protect her—to fight for her. But then he noticed most of the blood was coming from her nose. He knew all about her crack addiction.

"What's up?" he asked.

"I'm leaving."

"Oh, *o*-kay. So, um… where you goin'?"

"I mean, *I'm leaving,* Cody. I'm getting out of here. Out of this house, out of this city. Come with me. Let's do this together."

Cody looked behind her. He heard his father's pained groaning. The man retched and coughed, too. He nearly vomited due to the pain.

"Ahh, shit," Cody murmured. "What did you do this time?"

"I have to go soon," Crystal said. "You have to make your choice. A new life with me or the same shit with them. What's it going to be, kid?"

Cody chewed on his bottom lip. He wasn't prepared to make such a big decision. His brotherly instincts activated. He was a scrawny kid, skinny from a lack of food and bruised from his dad's beatings, but, once again, he felt an urge to protect his sister. He saw her as physically and mentally weak. He imagined she'd fall to prostitution if he didn't help her. It hurt him to see her like that.

He said, "I'll go. What do I need?"

"Your wallet. Your phone. That's it."

"I don't have any cash and my phone's dead. You know I don't have service."

"We can sell your phone and you just... you... you need a wallet, okay? Just get whatever you need and let's go."

Cody muttered to himself—*shit, fuck.* He grabbed his cell phone and his wallet. His wallet stored a collection of lint and his school ID. He followed his sister out of the room. He swallowed loudly upon spotting his injured father on the floor of Crystal's bedroom. He never expected her to fight back. They stopped in the living room.

Their mother, Diana Cox, sat on a recliner. Her arm was tied off above the peak of her bicep with a belt. A needle protruded from the crook of her elbow. Her drug of choice: *black tar heroin.* She was a frail, bony woman with pale skin. And her skin was blemished with track marks and severe acne. Her mouth hung open, revealing her broken, discolored, and even missing teeth.

She resembled a corpse, but she was breathing. Each breath was slow and raspy. She didn't notice her husband's bellows or her kids' desperate escape. She was gone.

Crystal pushed Cody and said, "She's fine. Go, go, go."

They ran out the front door. Cody sprinted to the red, beat-up muscle car in front of the small house. Crystal stopped on the porch.

She yelled, "Wait there!"

"What?! Where are you going?"

Crystal ran back to her room. She kicked her father's stomach. His weeping was interrupted by his coughing.

"You'll never hurt us again," she hissed as she kicked his face.

The tip of her shoe hit his left eye. A *pop* echoed through the room. The left side of his vision immediately blackened. The sclera of his eye changed from white to red—*apple-red.* His eyelids, bruised and irritated, slammed shut. A droplet of blood oozed out and rolled down his cheek, joining the tears and sweat on his face. He covered his face with one hand while covering his crotch with the other.

Crystal kicked his stomach again. The kick stopped him from screaming. He gasped for air and writhed in pain on the floor. Crystal grabbed her keys from the dresser, then she leaped across the bed and grabbed her trusty glass pipe. She growled as she kicked the back of her father's head, then she dashed out of the house. She met Cody at the car. They drove off, leaving a house of horrors behind them.

***

Jared Hatcher groaned as he awoke to the sound of knocking on the front door. Each knock sounded thunderous—*bang, bang, bang.* After a night of partying, his cocaine comedown left him with feelings of dysphoria, depression, agitation, and fatigue. He ran his fingers through his short black hair and sat up in bed.

"Who the hell are you?" he muttered.

A nude woman slept beside him. Tattoos decorated her arms and chest. Her nose, lips, and ears were pierced. Cocaine residue was powdered on her nose like makeup. A streak of dried semen clung to her curly hair. Jared was naked, too. He didn't remember the previous night, but the evidence suggested a cocaine sex party had occurred at the apartment.

Tap, tap, tap!

More knocking.

The twenty-one-year-old drug dealer stood up on his bed. He lunged over the unconscious woman, his flaccid dick swinging from side to side. He put on his boxers.

"Where is it?" he whispered as he kicked the dirty clothes covering the floor. He looked under the bed and said, "There you are, baby."

He stood up with a black pistol in his hand. He jumped back onto his bed and peeked out his window from behind the curtain. He lived on the second floor of an apartment building with exterior hallways. He couldn't see anyone outside. He didn't see any police cruisers or unmarked vehicles in the parking lot, so he eliminated the cops as a possibility. He crept over to his doorway.

"Mike," he whispered loudly. "Hey, Mikey! You hear that?"

Aside from the knocking, the home was quiet. He approached the room across the hall. Mike, his roommate, was unconscious on his king-sized bed, a naked woman at each side.

Jared muttered, "Dumbass..."

He tiptoed through the apartment. Trash flooded the home: garbage bags, pizza boxes, oyster pails, cigarette butts, used condoms, needles, burnt spoons, and even cartridge casings.

As he reached the living room, a woman outside shouted, "Jared! I know you're in there!" He recognized the voice. The woman knocked and yelled, "Open up! Jeez!"

Jared whispered, "Crystal, you bitch."

He was dating Crystal, although he saw a slew of other women on the side. He didn't trust Crystal, though. He didn't trust anyone as a matter of fact. The front door was riddled with bullet holes, which were now covered with pieces of cardboard. His home, known as a trap house, was frequently targeted by rival drug dealers, angry addicts, and police. It wouldn't have surprised him if Crystal betrayed him.

He peeked through the peephole and found the Cox siblings waiting for him outside. He put the pistol on the couch, then he opened the door just as Crystal was about to knock again. She missed him by an inch. He squinted as the sunshine attacked his jaundiced eyes.

Jared asked, "What are you doing here?"

"What took you so long?" Crystal asked.

"What do you think? I was sleeping."

"It's almost five, Jared!"

Jared grimaced and said, "Alright, whatever. Keep your voice down, will you?"

Crystal crossed her arms, rolled her eyes, and said, "You were sleeping with another dirty whore, weren't you? Where is she? Huh? In your bed? Is she high? You said you didn't have anymore–"

Cody tugged on her arm. He spoke with his sad, droopy eyes: *we're not here for that.* Crystal sighed in disappointment. She was ready to argue about drugs and women, but she fought to control herself. Jared smirked at them. He crossed his arms and legs while leaning against the doorway. Standing six-two, strong but malnourished, he towered over the siblings.

Crystal said, "I need your help. *We* need your help."

"What did you bring to my door this time, babe?"

"Not cops, not gangbangers. Nothing like that. We're running away."

Jared couldn't keep a straight face. *Running away*—as far as he knew, kids and teenagers ran away. Crystal was an adult, though.

He chuckled, then he asked, "*What?*"

"We're leaving Oro. I got in a fight with my dad and it's, um... It's just fucked up, okay? I got my car, I got a little bit of cash in my bank account, and I got a plan."

"Yeah? What's your plan? Let's hear it."

Cody sensed the arrogance in Jared's voice. He clenched his fists, but he bit his tongue. He never liked Jared. He blamed him for his sister's addiction. He guessed he sold the heroin to his mother, too.

Crystal said, "California. We have family there. Decent family. We'll live with our cousin for a while, then we'll rent our own place or something."

"That's not really a plan, Crystal," Jared said. "It's more like a... a hope. I mean, do you have enough gas money to get there? Do you even know if your 'decent' family gives a crap about you? What makes you think they won't call your dad? They never helped you before, did they?"

"Let me deal with that."

"Then what do you want from me?"

"A loan. Just enough for gas, some food, and maybe a few weeks at a cheap motel."

Jared puckered his lips and nodded. Although he

often cheated on her, he cared enough about her to call her his girlfriend. Their relationship would have had to end for Crystal to leave without him. And, if their relationship was over, he didn't see a reason to lend her any money.

"I don't know, babe," he said as he rubbed the two-inch scar on his neck. (A rival drug dealer attempted to slit his throat two years ago.) He said, "You want me to 'lend' you money so you can leave the state. That's pretty much what you're saying. And you know damn well you're not going to pay me back. So, where do *I* benefit?"

Crystal responded, "Please, Jared. I know I've asked you for money and drugs and *everything* before, but it's serious this time. My dad... He's going to kill me because I... I *fucked* him up. My brother won't make it far in this place, either. I love you. You *know* I love you, but I can't stay here anymore. Even with the drugs, I can't handle this pain. Help me."

Cody wanted to punch the smug smile off Jared's face. He knew he couldn't beat him in a fair fight, though. Violence rarely solved any of their problems anyway.

Jared sucked his teeth, then he said, "Alright, listen up and listen good. I wish I could help you, Crystal, but I don't have any extra cash."

"Bullshit," Crystal said, tears welling in her eyes. "You always have money. You're always showing off. You're loaded!"

"What did I say about keeping your voice down?"

Cody stepped forward and said, "Hey, man, you can't be talking to my sister like that. We're just trying–"

Crystal pressed her arm against Cody's chest and stopped him from approaching Jared. Jared scratched his hair and yawned.

He said, "Like I was saying, we got robbed a few nights ago." He tapped one of the holes on the door. He said, "They took our bread, our beans, our glass, our brown sugar... They took it all. They even shot one of my, um... 'roommates.' I don't know if he's dead or alive. And I have no idea if they're going to come knocking again."

Crystal asked, "Are you serious?"

"No lie."

Crystal staggered back until she crashed into the handrail behind her. She stared at the floor with a set of downcast eyes. She couldn't hold on to the little hope in her heart. Jared and Cody saw the unadulterated fear in her eyes. She had the eyes of someone facing death for the first time. She believed her dad would kill her if she returned home—if not today, tomorrow or the next day or the day after that.

Jared said, "I'll tell you what: I'll help you get your hands on some money if I can go with you."

Crystal furrowed her brow and asked, "You want to come with us?" Her eyes lit up and her lips shook with excitement. She said, "Really? Really-really?"

"Why?" Cody asked, equally baffled but less enthusiastic.

Jared said, "I need to get out of here, too, don't I? I'm not going to get shot by some bum-ass bitches."

Crystal asked, "So, how can we get some cash?"

"The same way they took mine. We'll rob someone, then we'll leave town. I know a guy with a cheap place in Vegas. Hear me out, alright? I know you want to get far from Oro, but I think it's better this way. There's no way your dad's going to find you in a city like Vegas, right? And staying in Vegas gives me sometime to finish up some deals and close some loose-ends. Then, I promise—*I cross my heart*—I'll take you to California and I'll set us up with an apartment. What do you say? It's better than living in some crappy motels or begging your cousin to help you out."

"I guess it can work."

Cody asked, "Are you sure about this, Crystal?"

Crystal sighed, then she said, "I don't know, but we don't have a lot of options. We can't go back. I know that for sure. I *won't* go back."

Jared said, "We'll make a plan tomorrow night. Where are you staying?"

"Well, I was hoping we could stay with you."

Jared said, "No, that's not going to work. There's no room and, uh…" He pointed at Cody and said, "I don't think this is the best 'environment' for the kid."

Cody responded, "I'm not a kid, man."

Ignoring him, Jared said, "Stay in your car somewhere or rent a room at the Gold Ranch Motel. It's cheap right now and I'll pay you back when we get to Vegas."

"Okay, so, um… I guess we'll stay at the motel," Crystal said.

"Great, I'll meet you there. Wait for me."

Before he could close it, Crystal put her palm on the door and her foot in the doorway. They locked eyes.

Crystal sniffled and asked, "Can you give me a rock?"

"I told you: I'm all out."

"Just one, Jared. Please."

"I'm out, but I'll try to bring something for you tomorrow. Alright?"

"O-Okay..."

Jared slammed the door, then he secured the locks. He grabbed his pistol and went back to his bedroom. He sat beside the nude woman. He retrieved a glass pipe and a rock of crack from a shoebox under his bed. He lay down and smoked it. The crack ignited his dormant libido. He rolled the unconscious woman onto her stomach, then he raped her.

Chapter Two

A Beautiful Life

In a dress and high heels, Shannon Cohen cooked pancakes at the stove. Her apron read: *World's Best Housewife!* Her brown hair—dyed by her eldest daughter—bounced with each peppy step. Her green eyes glowed like emeralds on piles of the whitest snow. At forty-five years old, she was in the prime of her life.

She flipped a pancake and shouted, "Breakfast is almost ready!"

"I'm starving!" Kimberly Cohen yelled from the dining table beyond the kitchen bar.

The thirteen-year-old girl doodled on an iPad while listening to music from one Bluetooth headphone. She drew *Pennywise the Dancing Clown*. She fell in love with the character after watching the latest adaptations of Stephen King's *It*. But, as a horror fan, she defied society's expectations by listening to pop music every day. Horror and pop—those were her favorite genres.

She sang: ♪ *Oh, baby, hold me closer! Don't tell me that it's over! 'Cause I know it ain't over!*

Jill Cohen, her eighteen-year-old sister, sat beside her. She typed away at her laptop, editing an essay for her senior English class. She was a star student and a popular softball player. She stood five-one—barely two inches taller than her little sister and five inches shorter than her mother—but she was strong and athletic. She had blue eyes, like her sister, sun-kissed skin, and voluminous brown hair.

Without taking her eyes off her screen, she yelled, "She's singing again! Please stop her!"

"I'm right here, Jill," Kimberly said. "You can tell me yourself."

"Fine, stop singing."

"You didn't say please. It's rude if you don't say please, you know."

Jill looked at her and said, "Please stop singing."

Kimberly sang: ♪ *No! No no! No no no no no!*

Jill grunted in frustration, then she said, "Mom, make her stop."

Shannon placed a plate of pancakes beside Jill's laptop and another next to Kimberly's iPad. Then she placed a butter dish and a glass bottle of organic maple syrup at the center of the table.

She said, "You should have finished your homework last night, hun, not during breakfast."

"It *is* finished. I'm just, you know, making it perfect."

Shannon snickered, then she said, "I know, I know. You're a perfectionist, just like your father when he was young." She sighed, then she pouted playfully. She said, "That's why my baby's going to university 'out-of-state.' All the way in California."

Kimberly giggled, then she said, "Jeez, mom, it's not *that* far."

"It is for a mother."

Jill said, "It's not like I'm leaving forever. Besides, Kim's right for once: it's really not that far."

Shannon shrugged, walked back to the kitchen, and said, "Great, gang up on me. I'm just the woman who cooks for you and cleans for you and loves you so very much."

"We love you, too!" Jill and Kimberly shouted in unison.

They all laughed. Jill and Kimberly set their differences aside and enjoyed their mother's fluffy pancakes while Shannon whipped up some more.

Patrick Cohen entered the living room from a hallway. He approached the seamlessly connected dining area while adjusting his tie.

"Good morning, ladies," he said as he walked past the dining table.

Again, in unison, his daughters said, "Good morning, dad."

Patrick grabbed Shannon's hips and kissed her cheek. Even when she wore heels, he stood a few inches taller than his wife. He was a forty-six-year-old physician. His grizzled hair was slicked back. The sleeves of his dress shirt were rolled up, revealing his hairy forearms. Bushy eyebrows sprouted above his expensive Tom Ford prescription glasses.

He said, "Smells great."

"It's just pancakes, hun," Shannon responded as she flipped another one.

"I was talking about you," Patrick said with a sly smirk.

"*Oh*, shut up."

"It's true."

Giggling, Shannon said, "Sit down. I'll serve you in a minute."

"Thanks," Patrick said before kissing her again. He went past the kitchen bar and returned to the dining area. Along with Kimberly, he sang: ♪ *Don't tell me that it's over! 'Cause I know it ain't over!*

Kimberly stopped singing. She raised her brow at him, then she looked away awkwardly. She loved teasing him because of his awful singing. Jill covered her mouth as she laughed.

Patrick asked, "What's the matter, honey? I thought we were having a sing-along party?"

"Party's over," Kimberly responded. She chuckled and said, "You can't sing, dad. We've been through this before."

"At least you got her to stop," Jill said before stuffing another forkful of pancakes into her mouth.

Patrick ruffled Kimberly's hair and said, "Don't worry about her. I know you still love singing with your old man."

Kimberly smiled as she poured some more syrup on her pancakes. As a matter of fact, she loved singing with her father. Her wavy hair stuck out in every direction, but she didn't care.

Jill held her hands over her head as her father walked behind her. She said, "Please don't mess up my hair. It took all morning and I don't want to do it again." Patrick reached for her head, teasing her. She said, "Please, dad. I'm serious."

"Alright, alright," Patrick responded. He sat down at the other end of the table. He said, "But we have to talk about your makeup. It's not Halloween yet, sweetheart. You shouldn't have your face caked like that."

"*Caked?*" Jill repeated, trying to hold her laughter. She said, "I barely put anything on."

Shannon placed a plate of pancakes in front of her husband and said, "She's right. It's not that much, hun."

"She looks beautiful, dad," Kimberly said, focusing on her meal.

Patrick said, "It's always the boys against the girls, isn't it? Where's my backup?" He looked at the empty seats, then he glanced over at the hallway. He asked, "Where's Dustin?"

Shannon said, "I tried to wake him, but he said he didn't have class today, so he wants to sleep in."

"Sleep in? No one sleeps in around here. He should be having breakfast with us."

"I know. I told him that, but the boy's tired, Pat."

"If he's going to be living here, he needs to at least *act* like he's part of this family. It's good to have a schedule, too. You know what they say: the early bird catches the worm."

Mouth full of pancakes, Kimberly said, "*But,* the early worm is *caught* by the bird."

Jill rolled her eyes and said, "That was such a geek thing to say."

While the girls argued, Patrick moseyed down the hall and headed to Dustin's room. Dustin Cohen slept with his back to the door. Shadows swallowed every corner of his bedroom. There was a backpack on the floor near the foot of the bed, surrounded by dirty laundry and empty water bottles. Six thick textbooks—covering subjects from English to business—sat on his desk.

He attended a community college in Las Vegas. His parents had saved thousands of dollars to send him to any college in the country, but his poor grades held him back. He planned on transferring to a different school and moving away from home after completing his second year. He loved his family, he cared about them, but he saw them as phonies—fakes, *actors.*

The 'perfect' family was a myth, and he wanted no part of it.

Patrick approached his son. He opened the curtains over the bed and welcomed a wave of sunshine into the room. Dustin groaned as he rolled over. He scratched his scruffy hair and squinted.

"What time is it?" he asked in a drowsy voice.

"It's time to get up."

Dustin's blurred vision adjusted and he finally recognized his father. He sat up in bed and watched as his dad flipped through his textbooks, lips sinking in disappointment.

"I don't have class today," Dustin said.

"It doesn't matter, Dustin. What have I always told you? If you want to succeed, you have to be *pro*-active. You have to get yourself out there. You're twenty years old now. You're not supposed to wait until the last minute to do your homework or wake up after lunch. You have to stay focused, you have to... You have to be punctual, you understand?"

Irritated, Dustin repeated, "I *don't* have class today."

"I get that. I'm not telling you to go to school. I'm asking you to get up and do something... positive or... or beneficial. And you can start by having a wholesome breakfast with your family."

Dustin always felt unappreciated by his father, especially compared to his sisters. He was treated like a failure, so he felt like a massive disappointment. But he held back. Arguing with his father was like debating a contemporary politician—pointless because he would never listen. He wanted to live rent-free, save his money, and move out as soon as possible without causing any other problems.

He nodded and said, "I'll be out in a minute."

Patrick asked, "You have plans for Halloween?"

Sitting at the edge of his bed, Dustin put on his sweatpants and said, "I don't have class if that's what you're asking."

"So what are you doing?"

"You know what I'm doing. I'm going to the Halloween party at *Oro Center*. Everyone's going."

"You go ahead and do that, but, since you don't have class, I want you to put in some hours at the homeless shelter before you head out."

The Cohen family was known for volunteering and donating—from helping out at homeless shelters to cleaning up parks, from donating cash to donating blood. Patrick enjoyed helping people and he believed it was a beneficial addition to his children's résumés. Dustin didn't see a difference between his father and people on social media performing good deeds in exchange for virtual 'likes.'

Dustin said, "I was going to meet up with Natalie before the party."

Patrick responded, "Well, meet her at the homeless shelter." He noticed the frustration in his son's eyes. He said, "Listen, Jill already worked her ass off out there. They know her on first name basis at the shelter. You? You haven't been down there in a while. You have to stay fresh on their minds if you want them to support you. You scratch their back, they'll scratch yours. That's how the world works."

"I get it. How long?"

"They need someone from four to eight. You can

head to the party after that. Deal?"
"Deal."
"Attaboy. Now let's get some breakfast. Your mom made pancakes."
"*Great,*" Dustin said in a sarcastic tone.

Chapter Three

The Plan

"This place is a dump," Jared said as he walked into the motel room.

Beige wallpaper with brown pinstripes covered the walls, stained and peeling. Between the foot of the bed and the dresser, the red carpet was spattered with dark stains. Piles of dust peppered with insect droppings accumulated in the corners of the room. It was 2019, but a bulky tube television sat atop the dresser. There was a king-sized bed to the left, the sheets disheveled and discolored. The bathroom at the other end of the room didn't fare much better, but at least the plumbing worked.

Crystal closed and locked the door behind him, then she leaned back against the wall. She shivered, but the room wasn't cold. She was crashing due to the lack of crack in her system. Jared peeked out the window and checked the parking lot outside, as if he were expecting someone to follow him. The shooting at his apartment, along with his drug abuse, left him perpetually paranoid. He set his backpack down on the bed beside Cody, who watched a fuzzy episode of *Family Guy* on the television.

Jared sat down on a seat in the corner of the room and sighed. Except for the sound of Seth MacFarlane voicing every character on the TV, the room was quiet.

Crystal shrugged and said, "Well? What are we waiting for? Are we going to rob someone or what?"

"Calm down, baby," Jared responded. "We're not robbing anyone tonight."

"Excuse me? What do you mean by that? I–I thought you had a–a–a plan. You said you had a plan yesterday, Jared!"

"Jesus, Crystal, I told you to calm down, didn't I?"

His eyes on the television, Cody said, "She wouldn't be like that if you didn't get her hooked on that crap."

Crystal snapped, "Oh, shut up, brat!"

"Why are you screaming at me? I'm on your side."

"Oh, *please!* No one's on my side! I–I'm going crazy over here and none of you are–"

"Shut up!" Jared barked. Crystal clenched her jaw and swallowed the lump in her throat. Jared nodded at Cody and said, "Turn that shit off."

Cody turned off the television. He felt the animosity in Jared's voice. Crystal felt it, too. She sat down at the foot of the bed, breathing deeply through her nose. They sat in silence for a minute.

Elbows on his knees, Jared leaned forward and said, "Let's get some things straight. If this is going to work, we won't be screaming and we won't be using any cell phones. That means no calls, no text messages, no emails. I don't want anyone to link this back to us. No one can ever know about this. *No one.* Alright?"

The siblings nodded.

Jared continued, "Good. *If this is going to work,* we need a plan. I never said I had one, Crystal, I said we'd work on one. But, I do have some ideas. You wanna hear 'em or are you just going to scream and bitch again?"

Crystal stuttered, "I–I won't scream. I'm just

feeling a–a little sick."

"Your brother's right. You're just going through withdrawals. You've been through it before, so just get over it until we deal with it later. Now let's get down to business. The idea is the same: we're going to rob someone. I'm not talking about some random strangers on the streets. We won't get far stealing wallets and cell phones. No, we're going to pick a *family* tomorrow. A rich family. A *filthy* rich family. We'll hold 'em up at their house on Halloween."

Cody stuttered, "A–A home invasion?"

"That's right."

"On Halloween?" Crystal said, doubt in her voice. "Why not tonight? I need to get outta here, Jared. I really, really need to get the hell outta *Oro*."

Jared leaned back in his seat and said, "I know I'm not the smartest guy around. I'm not like your little brother or those rich college kids, but when it comes down to this... I'm not stupid. I know how to make it work and *this* is how it's going to work. Think about it. Everyone's going to the big Halloween party at Oro Center on Thursday night. That means, most people will be busy there, so the *cops* will be busy there. That also means we have a reason to wear disguises. We could walk around in ski masks and no one would notice us. It's perfect, right? *Right?*"

The siblings looked at each other, surprised. Like Crystal, Jared was a high school dropout and a drug addict—and he was also a drug dealer. He didn't make many smart decisions in his life. But his idea was thought-out. He knew how to rob people while minimizing the risks. He studied past criminals and learned from his peers. He was an intelligent young man, but his nihilism led him down a road of deviance and despair.

Cody wondered if Jared had robbed families before using similar methods. *A Halloween tradition?*–he thought.

Cody asked, "But what's the difference between robbing random people and rich families? I mean, we still have to sell their shit, right? Like jewelry and all that?"

Jared said, "We'll steal some of their shit, sure. Might as well, right? But that's not the... the 'main course.' No, I was thinking we'd do something different. We pick a rich family, right? Then we break into their house while they're home. We hold most of them hostage, except for maybe the mom. Then one of us will go out with mama bear and head to a bank. We'll force her to withdraw the maximum amount. And she'll have to do it 'cause the rest of us will be home with her family. If anything goes wrong... *you know.*"

"You–You'll hurt them?"

"It won't come to that because of, uh... our suggestion, *our threat*. Yeah, she won't say 'no' because she'll be too scared for her family. We won't really have to hurt any of them while she's withdrawing the cash."

Cody nodded. He stared at the reflection on the television. They looked like warped versions of themselves—distorted, bloated, stretched shadows. In that motel room, as they planned the robbery of an innocent family, the darkness consumed them. They were inching towards the point of no return.

Crystal said, "Okay, o–okay. So, then... we have to,

um..." She squeezed her eyes shut and shook her head, trying to clear her cloudy mind. She said, "We have to catch them while the bank is still open. So it has to be around sundown, right when it's getting dark."

"That's right, baby," Jared said. "In that bag, I have a pistol and some heroin. We'll use the pistol to scare 'em. I was thinking we could inject 'em with some heroin after we finished. We'll let 'em nod off and, if they're the snobby, stuck-up type, they might not even report us after we're finished. They'll be too embarrassed. Shame... it's worse than bullets for some people. Shit's crazy, isn't it?"

He glanced around the room and thought about his own words. He never blackmailed anyone before, but it seemed like a profitable business.

Crystal asked, "Who's our mark? We can't rob anyone that's *too* rich 'cause they'll probably have security, right?"

Jared pushed the curtain aside, peeked out the window, and said, "You're right again. We'll stay away from politicians and gated communities. We'll have to pick someone out tomorrow, so we'll have to check out a few neighborhoods and maybe follow a couple of people. Until then, let's just relax here." He closed the curtain. He smirked at Crystal and said, "Let's mess around."

Crystal's lips twitched as she glanced over at her younger brother. Cody grimaced in disgust and shook his head, as if to say: *not in front of me, please.*

Crystal stuttered, "I–I can't..."

"Why not?" Jared asked. "Don't tell me it's 'cause of your brother. He's not a little kid, Crystal. He's probably seen more porn than both of us combined."

"But–but he's my brother..."

Jared responded, "So? Everyone's watching that fake incest porn these days anyway." He looked at Cody and said, "Pretend like you're watching some live porn. It's just, uh, you know... a play."

Cody shook his head and said, "I don't want to see that."

"Then watch TV, close your eyes, go to sleep, or leave. You've got a lot of options, kid, but cock-blocking ain't one of 'em."

Jared sat beside Crystal. He rubbed her back with one hand and her thigh with the other. Cody scooted to the other side of the bed. He looked away from them, hoping to hear another rejection from his sister.

Jared said, "Come on, babe. I need this if I'm going to be focused."

"Jared, I–I don't know. Why don't we just go to the pool or something? I need some fresh air or a swim."

"You know I can't swim. Come on, let's do this."

"But I–I'm... I'm sick. I just can't do it right now."

"You can. *You will.*"

Tears rolling down her cheeks and voice trembling, Crystal said, "I'm really feeling sick."

Jared stopped massaging her and glared at her with smoldering eyes. Crystal recognized that look of rage in his eyes. *Just like dad's,* she thought. But she wasn't scared of him. She was aroused by his anger—by his abuse. It was called 'trauma bonding.' The cycle of punishment-and-reward filled her with cortisol and dopamine. It sent her to the deepest lows and the tallest highs.

Jared grunted to clear his throat, then he reached into his backpack. He pulled a small baggie out. On top of a line of white crumbs, there were two off-white rocks inside it—gravel, candy, *crack.*

"Oh God," Crystal said, smiling. Her tears of anxiety turned into tears of joy in an instant. She grabbed her crack pipe from the dresser. She said, "Finally."

Jared broke one of the rocks. He packed it into her pipe, then he handed her a lighter. Her hands trembled as she lit it. The stench of crack—like burning plastic and nail polish—immediately stained the room. The rush of euphoria flowed through her within seconds. She tried to take another hit, scraping at the bottom of her pipe.

Jared took the pipe out of her hands and said, "Let's fuck."

"*Let's fuck,*" Crystal repeated as she nodded and giggled.

They kissed while tugging on each other's clothes. Jared fell back on the bed as he removed his shirt. Crystal licked his nipple as she took off her jeans and panties. She forgot about her socks. Jared pushed her head down to his crotch. Crystal pulled his pants and boxers down to his ankles, then she slurped his erect penis into her mouth. She kept the glans in her mouth while stroking the shaft. Her breasts bounced up and down with each quick bob of her head. Without taking his dick out of her mouth, she crawled over him, turned around, and then sat on his face. Jared spread her ass and licked her from her clitoral hood to her anus.

Cody hopped off the bed. He stepped back into a corner, mouth ajar. In a matter of seconds, his sister changed from agitated to horny. Crack cocaine was a powerful aphrodisiac. He covered his ears with his palms and lurched towards the bathroom. Before he could reach the door, he heard his sister's loud, sultry moan through his hands. A thin wall and a flimsy door couldn't protect him from the sounds of crackhead sex. With his head down, he ran to the front door. From the corner of his eye, he saw his sister preparing to ride Jared in the reverse cowgirl position, slapping her labia with the tip of his dick. He could only shudder as he stumbled out of the room.

He slammed the door behind him, then he jogged into the parking lot. He put twenty meters of distance between himself and the room, but he swore he could still hear Crystal's moaning. He dug his fingers into his hair and walked in circles at the center of the parking lot. Tears trickled from his eyes. He muttered to himself about Crystal and their family, Jared and his plan, life and its hardships. He stopped and faced the building.

He stomped and shouted, "Fuck! Fuck me! I don't want to do this! I just want it all to go away!" He stared up at the night sky and yelled, "Why me?! Why did you make my life like this?!"

There was no response. There was no divine intervention. He didn't hear the voice of God. His sister and her boyfriend continued to have sex in the motel room, unaware of his fear, his doubt, and his suffering. Cody stood by his lonesome in the parking lot. He was surrounded by vehicles, dozens of people slept in the building in front of him, but he felt like the last person on Earth. He was abandoned.

Chapter Four

Scouting

Cody stood on his tiptoes and looked over a gate at the side of a two-story house. In the narrow space between the brick wall and the house, he saw a small storage shed, a dusty grill, a stack of patio chairs, and some gardening tools. He spotted the trimmed grass in the backyard, too. He pulled the hood of his sweater over his head and walked onto the front porch. He held his hand over his mouth upon noticing the doorbell camera.

"Shit," he muttered.

He examined the couch and rocking chair. The furniture looked expensive—sturdy, *antique.* He weaved and bobbed his head as he tried to look through the sidelights. He narrowed his eyes. Inside, there was a large rectangular shape on the wall to his left, but he couldn't make it out. A picture frame? A painting? Either way, he equated decorations with wealth. The doorbell camera forced him to question the home's security system, though.

Just as he reached the bottom of the porch steps, the front door swung open. He froze with his back to the door. He thought about running, but he didn't want to arouse more suspicion.

From the doorway, a man asked, "Can I help you?"

Cody glanced over his shoulder, doe-eyed. The man was old, bald with a white goatee. He looked healthy, he could walk on his own without a limp, but the group of desperadoes could have easily overpowered him. Behind the old man, he saw an entrance hall decorated with paintings at each side. A diagonal gallery of picture frames ran up the stairs. Some of the photos were in black-and-white. He was the perfect target.

Trying to keep his head low, Cody returned to the porch and stuttered, "He–Hey, um... I was just, uh..."

"Go on," the man said, his brow raised in confusion.

"I'm volunteering for the church and we're just asking for donations for... for the homeless shelter and the food drive."

"Which church?"

"The, um... The Church of Christ?" Cody responded, a hint of doubt in his voice.

"Is that your answer or a question, son?"

"A–An answer. I'm here for the Church of Christ."

The man wagged his cell phone at him and said, "I saw you through the app. Through the camera right there." He pointed at the doorbell. He asked, "You were prowling, weren't you?"

"I wasn't. I was just... I was... I was ashamed to ask for help. I got cold feet, okay? I really am looking for donations. I'm sorry if I scared you or anything like that."

The man analyzed Cody from head-to-toe. He didn't see a thug on his porch. He saw a frail, pale teenager. He didn't believe his lies about the church, but he saw the unmistakable glaze of shame in his eyes. He glanced around the neighborhood. There were no suspicious people or vehicles in sight. He took a twenty dollar bill out of his wallet and handed it to Cody.

As Cody accepted the money, the man said, "Don't

use this on drugs."

"Yeah, I won't."

"Stay out of trouble, son."

"Tha–Thank you."

The man closed the door. Cody heard the locks *clicking* and *clacking*, but he didn't hear any footsteps beyond the door. The homeowner was already suspicious, watching him through the peephole.

Cody walked past the front gate. He strolled past the neighbor's house, acting calm and natural, then he sped up. With each passing house, he walked faster. He jogged around the corner of the block, then he went into an alley behind the last house. Crystal's red muscle car was parked behind a dumpster. Jared sat in the driver's seat and Crystal slept in the passenger seat with her arms crossed.

Jared climbed out, adjusted the chair, and let Cody into the backseat. Then he hopped back into the car. He watched Cody through the rear-view mirror.

Cody patted Jared's shoulder and said, "Let's go. This place is a bust."

"What do you mean it's 'a bust?' Those were some nice houses, kid," Jared said as he drove down the alley.

"They weren't bad. It's just, um…"

"What happened?"

"I found a pretty nice house. It looked empty, so I took a look around. I checked the porch for cameras, like you told me to, but… Well, this guy had a camera on his doorbell. He caught me before I could leave. He told me he saw me through an app on his phone. I don't know if he recorded me, but he definitely saw me. I'm sorry, man."

"*Shit!* You fucking retard!"

Crystal hopped in her seat, startled by the sudden screaming. She glanced around, eyes bulging from her head as if she had awoken in a different car in a different city surrounded by different men.

Cody said, "I lied to him. I told him I was asking for donations for church."

"Did he believe you? Cody, did he believe you or not?"

"He did. I mean, I think he did. He gave me twenty dollars."

He pulled the money out of his pocket and showed it to them. With cat-like reflexes, Crystal yanked it out of his hand. *Crack money*—that was all she saw.

As he cruised out of the neighborhood, Jared said, "You could have fucked us, kid. You need to be more careful. I won't hesitate to drop your ass if you fuck up again."

Drop your ass—Cody couldn't tell if he was threatening to kick him off their little team, knock him out cold, or kill him. They drove towards the center of the city—Oro City's shopping district.

Breaking the silence while looking out his window, Cody asked, "Why can't we just rob one of your friends? Like a drug dealer or a gang banger or something like that? You know them better than anyone, right? We can take their money and run away."

Jared huffed, then he said, "You really are a fucking retard, aren't you?"

"I'm just saying. It's safer than robbing innocent–"

"You don't know shit, kid," Jared interrupted. "You don't play with a drug dealer's money unless you have a *reason* to fuck with 'em... or a death wish. There are levels to all this shit, you see? That drug dealer you want to rob, he's probably at the bottom of the pyramid. His bosses are going to want that money. You know who their bosses are?"

Cody stayed silent.

Jared said, "They're dangerous drug lords who don't appreciate it when people take their money. We're talking about cartel bosses, mob bosses, shit like that. These people will *torture* you, kid. They'll skin you alive. They'll take your–your *organs* out of your body and feed 'em to you. They'll blow you to *bits* with dynamite. They'll cut your head off with a butter knife, kid!"

Cody clenched his jaw and drew a deep breath through his nose, unnerved by the descriptions of violence. Jared spoke as if he had experienced it all before.

"You want to play with their money? Be my guest, but I'm not that stupid. Nah, not me," Jared continued. "Rich people have insurance, Cody. Rich people aren't going to retaliate, *Cody.* That's why we have to do it this way. I know you're scared, you don't want to break the law or hurt any 'innocent' people, but don't forget: *no one* is innocent here. They got rich by stepping on people like us, and that's the truth. Think of it as... as us taking back what's ours."

Cody didn't share Jared's beliefs. He wasn't a hopeless optimist, but he wasn't an apathetic nihilist, either. He landed somewhere in the middle. He was jealous of the rich families in Oro City, but he didn't hate them enough to wish harm on them. He focused on his own survival while attempting to protect his sister.

He said, "I just don't want anyone to get hurt over this. I wish there was an easier way."

Crystal said, "This *is* the easiest way, brat. Besides, it's not like anyone's going to die. They'll get their money back from their insurance companies and their bruises will get better in a couple of days. It'll be like nothing ever happened."

I don't think we can do this—Cody wanted to say those words, but he gritted his teeth and withdrew from the conversation. Jared was a violent criminal, Crystal was an unstable drug addict, and *he* was a cowardly teenager. Their gang wasn't ready to rob a family.

Jared parked outside of a grocery store. He said, "We need a break and I'm starving. Go in there and buy some food."

"What?" Crystal asked.

"You heard me, babe. I'm in the mood for some... some rotisserie chicken and potato salad. Grab me a Coke while you're in there, too."

"Are you serious?"

"No shit, Crystal. Just go in there and buy some damn food already."

Crystal held her hand out in front of Jared.

Jared slapped it away and said, "Use the twenty."

Glaring at him, Crystal said, "I was going to use that–"

"*Use the twenty,*" Jared repeated, raising his voice. He returned the glare and said, "Or pay with your debit card. Go."

"Whatever," Crystal said. She climbed out of the car and said, "Let's go, Cody."

As Cody exited the car, Jared shouted, "And keep an eye out for some game!"

***

The shopping cart—stocked with a small rotisserie chicken, a container of potato salad, and three twenty-ounce bottles of Coke—*squealed* and *rattled* gratingly as Crystal pushed it down an aisle. One of the wheels spun in every direction, forcing her to readjust her direction repeatedly. Cody followed her, leering at the food like a pervert ogling young women at a mall. He was starving.

Cody said, "I know you've been with him for a few years, but... why do you let him treat you like a... like a..."

"A crackhead?" Crystal asked without looking back.

"No, like a slave. We're in here buying him food with our money while he's sleeping in the car. He didn't pay for the motel room, either. He hasn't paid for shit, Crystal. He hasn't done shit, either. He came up with the plan, but we could have done that ourselves. You're paying for everything, I'm scouting the houses and–"

"Keep your voice down, brat," Crystal interrupted.

Cody sucked his lips and glanced around. They strolled down an aisle of condiments, crackers, and potato chips. An elderly woman read the expiration date on each bottle of ketchup.

He walked closer to Crystal and said, "I'm just saying, he should help out, too. It's not fair."

"Let's get some things straight, Cody. *You* didn't pay for anything, either. You looked at a few places, so what? The motel, the gas, the food... It's *my* money,

40   Jon Athan

and he's my boyfriend, so it's fair."

And you'll do anything for his crack and cock—again, he stopped himself from blurting out that response. He saw her as a selfish, self-destructive woman—the type of person who would throw him under the bus at the first sign of trouble—but he couldn't abandon her. He remembered his eleventh birthday. His sister took him away from their broken home. They watched *Jurassic World* at a movie theater, then they snuck into a screening of *Ted 2*. She paid for the popcorn and the Buncha Crunch—which they mixed together—and their drinks.

He walked beside her with his head down, like a child scolded for asking for candy. As they exited the aisle, another cart crashed into theirs.

A girl said, "*Oops.*"

"Oh, I'm so sorry," a woman said. "Kimmy, I told you to push the cart, not play on your phone."

Cody emerged from the aisle, eyes narrowed in curiosity. Around the corner, Shannon and Kimberly Cohen stood beside the other cart. Kimberly had been pushing the cart while fiddling with her cell phone. Like most teenagers, the phone was practically grafted to her hand. Shannon walked beside her, tossing groceries into the cart as they browsed. They shopped for baking materials, including piping bags and icing tips. Kimberly wanted to bake cookies to decorate them as the heads of iconic horror movie characters.

Crystal clenched her jaw and tightened her grip on the handle of her cart. Yet again, the lack of crack cocaine in her system left her agitated and unstable.

Through her gritted teeth, she growled, "*It's fine.*"

Kimberly backed up, face scrunched up in fear. She was young and naïve, so she subconsciously judged people based on their appearances. Crystal was nineteen years old, but she looked older than Shannon because of her drug abuse. Cody—pale, skinny, and wearing black from head-to-toe with his hood over his head—resembled a cliché school shooter. She took a few more steps back until she found cover behind her mother.

Shannon smiled at the teenagers and said, "You two have a nice day."

Crystal scowled at her. She saw a selfish, arrogant, and wealthy woman with a spoiled daughter. *They think they're better than us,* she told herself, *they deserve to get robbed.* Cody saw something different. He felt the sincerity behind Shannon's smile, he saw the compassion in her glimmering eyes. Kimberly watched them with a hint of suspicion in her eyes, but Cody understood her reaction. If the shoe were on the other foot, he wouldn't have trusted himself or his sister, either.

Trying to defuse the situation, Cody stuttered, "You–You, too."

Shannon and Kimberly went on their way. Crystal followed the rattling of their cart while keeping some distance between them.

In a soft voice, just above a whisper, Cody said, "I know her."

"For real?" Crystal asked without taking her eyes off the Cohens.

"Yeah, I know them. They're, um... They live over at the cul-de-sac. Yeah, yeah, I know their other daughter, Jill. I mean, I never really said anything to her, but she's a senior at my school. Jill Cohen, that's her name."

"Did it look like she recognized you?"

"No, I don't think so. I've never said a word to her. I saw her with Jill at one of the food drives once. Jill was, you know, volunteering or something."

"They're rich, aren't they?"

"I guess so."

"She looks like one of those rich cunts. Fucking show-off."

Cody was caught off guard by his sister's vulgar language. He heard worse before, but he didn't expect her to say it out loud in a grocery store. The siblings followed the Cohens to the checkout area at the front of the store. They ended up behind Shannon and Kimberly in line. Kimberly side-eyed them, watching as they unloaded their cart and placed their food on the checkout counter's conveyer belt.

Crystal leaned over her cart and stared at Shannon, estimating the value of her outfit. Flower-shaped diamond earrings from Tiffany & Co.? *At least a grand,* she thought. A diamond engagement ring and a wedding band? *A few more grand,* she figured. The expensive dress, the beautiful heels, the smartwatch? *This bitch is wearing thousands on her,* she thought. Her eyes widened as Shannon pulled a Louis Vuitton wallet out of her matching bag. She didn't travel with a lot of cash, but she had at least six credit cards in her wallet.

After paying for their items, Shannon and Kimberly loaded their cart again. Shannon gave Cody a nod and a smile. Then they left the store.

"Hurry up," Crystal said to the clerk as she leaned

to her right and watched her targets exit the building. She beckoned to Cody and said, "Go to the car. I'll meet you there."

Cody understood her instructions. His sister didn't want to lose the Cohens, so she wanted her brother to catch a glimpse of their vehicle before they departed. Cody walked briskly out of the store. Hands in his pockets, he walked across the parking lot and glanced around while trying to act natural. He spotted Shannon and Kimberly behind a black luxury SUV, loading their items into the trunk. He thought about helping them out of the kindness of his heart, but he knew it would only cause trouble in the future. He tried to bury his conscience, but, like a zombie, it kept rising from its grave.

He moseyed over to Crystal's car. He sat in the backseat and sighed. Jared glanced over at him, then he looked around the parking lot.

He asked, "Where's your sister?"

"She's coming."

"Yeah? Why are you here without her?"

"We, um... We have a 'target' or whatever."

"Who?"

Cody leaned over the center console, pointed at the SUV as it reversed out of the parking space, and said, "There."

"Shit, they're already leaving," Jared said as he turned the key in the ignition. "Where the fuck is your sister?"

A minute later, the passenger door swung open. Crystal entered the car with two bags of groceries. Jared peeled out of the parking space.

He asked, "What the hell took you so long?"

"I had to pay for the food, asshole," Crystal said. "They would have gotten suspicious if I just left and followed them."

"And now we lost 'em. Shit, you idiots..."

"We didn't lose 'em," Crystal said. She looked back at her brother and asked, "You said they lived at the cul-de-sac, right?"

Cody nodded.

Crystal said, "And you saw their car, right?'

Cody nodded again.

Crystal smirked and said, "Then we'll go to the cul-de-sac. If their car is there, then we've got our target. If it's not, then it was probably some bitch and her kid from one of those penthouses. We couldn't rob them anyway."

Jared spun the steering wheel and took a right out of the parking lot. They cruised over to the cul-de-sac at the edge of the city. The houses in the neighborhood were surrounded by white picket fences and separated by wide gaps of empty space. Beyond the houses on each side of the street, a sea of desert stretched beyond the horizon. Some of the homes were decorated as haunted houses.

Plastic headstones stood on the freshly-cut lawns. Decals of shadowy monsters clung to some of the windows. Dozens of pale arms protruded from the walls of an open garage. There was a fog machine on one of the driveways, ready to emit clouds of water-based fog at the front lawn. Fake spiders and thick cobwebs hung from the trees. And, of course, jack-o'-lanterns sat on every porch.

Jared muttered, "This place is like a movie, unreal..."

He made a U-turn at the end of the cul-de-sac. He grinned as he spotted the SUV from the grocery store. He sped away from the house before the Cohens could recognize their stalking behavior.

"They're perfect," he said. "We're going to make a lot of money off them. Good fuckin' job."

"Thanks," Crystal said, shivering in the passenger seat. "Can I have a hit now? Please?"

"You'll get another hit when we get home."

"I need it now. I'll be quick."

"Don't ask me again, baby. You know I don't like repeating myself."

While they argued, Cody turned and looked out the rear window. The house at the dead-end shrank until it vanished from his vision. He didn't want to rob them, but he knew he couldn't talk Jared and Crystal out of it. The Cohens were unaware of the crosshairs on their backs—unaware of the hellish experience planned for their Halloween night.

Chapter Five

Practice Makes Perfect

"Keep it down, alright?" Jared whispered. "Mikey doesn't know about any of this and he doesn't need to know about it."

"I just want to smoke," Crystal said with a low, drowsy voice.

Cody followed them down the hall of Jared's apartment, trying to navigate the darkness while stepping over the trash. Jared entered his bedroom and threw his backpack on his bed. Crystal scanned the dresser, the nightstand, and the floor, searching for the smallest grain of crack in the dark. The sound of creaky floorboards wafted through the trap house.

Cody peeked into the bedroom across from Jared's. He spotted Mikey, Jared's drug-dealing roommate, lying in bed. Brown vomit stained his lips, cheeks, and chin. He was motionless, fingers interlocked over his flat abdomen. The room reeked, contaminated with the combined stench of feces, urine, dirty laundry, crack smoke, and vinegar.

The young teenager turned his attention to Jared's room. He stood in the doorway and watched as his sister desperately searched for a rock of crack. He glanced over at Jared.

Jared knelt beside his bed, like a child praying before sleep. He stored his supplies under the bed: a machete with a fifteen-inch blade, a pocket knife, a crowbar, bolt-cutters, a hammer, an aluminum baseball bat, and baggies filled with marijuana, black tar heroin, and crack cocaine. He shoved a handful of baggies into his backpack and left the rest behind in the shoebox. He placed his tools in the backpack, except the baseball bat.

He opened a drawer on the dresser. Under the dirty, torn socks, he found a partially used roll of duct tape.

He muttered, "Shit, it's not enough." He wagged the roll at Cody and said, "Remind me to buy some more before tomorrow night."

Cody watched as Jared drew his handgun from the back of his waistband and checked the magazine. He couldn't say a word. He was paralyzed by his fear. *If no one's supposed to get hurt,* he thought, *why do you need so many weapons?* He had seen handguns before, every cop had one in their holsters, but he never saw a pistol in a criminal's hand.

He stuttered, "I–I, um, thought we weren't going to hurt anyone."

"We said no one was going to die."

"You have a... a gun, man."

"What? You think I'm going to shoot them? What did I tell you, kid? I said I'm *not* an idiot. I'm not going to shoot them, but I'm not going to let them shoot me, either. We don't know if these people are the stand-your-ground type of motherfuckers. I'm going to protect myself, your sister, and *you.* That's why we need the gun. Do you have a problem with that?"

Cody shook his head. He accepted Jared's excuse concerning the pistol. It was smart, it was logical. He was skeptical of the blades and blunt weapons, though.

He asked, "What about the knife? The machete?

The bat? What do we need all that for?"

Jared chuckled and facepalmed. He said, "This thing isn't going to happen in five minutes. Not fifteen. Not thirty. This is going to take over an hour. Maybe two. You said this is a family of four—*at the minimum.* One of us is leaving to the bank with mama, so that means two of us have to take care of three of them. If we go in there with one gun and they get ballsy, they'll just rush me and then what? I either shoot them or it's game over. Listen, Cody, we have to *take* control and *keep* control to make this work." He held the backpack up and said, "That's what this is for. This is our insurance."

Cody nodded. It made sense after all. Jared saw the reluctance in Cody's eyes. He saw a younger version of himself—a shy, untainted kid.

He handed Cody the baseball bat and said, "Follow me."

"Where are we going?"

As she looked through the closet, Crystal said, "Wait for me. Wait, I–I'm coming."

They entered Mike's bedroom. The drug dealer snored and twitched. He survived his drug binge, but he dragged himself to the brink of death—while also soiling himself.

Jared said, "Cave his head in."

Cody stepped back and laughed nervously, as if to say: *you're kidding, right?* Jared kept a steady face. He pushed him towards Mike's bed. Cody looked back at him, then at his sister, and then at Mike. His lips trembled while his limbs shook.

"Cave his head in," Jared repeated. "Go ahead. He isn't going to fight back. Look at him, kid. He's knocked out cold. And no one's going to give a shit if he dies. We both know that. So, do it."

"Wh–Why?"

"You need to learn how to defend yourself. If shit goes down, I need to know that you've got my back. Come on, kid, you know what they say: practice makes perfect. Now... *Cave. His. Head. In.*"

From the hall, Crystal said, "Leave him alone. Come on, he's just–"

"If you want another hit tonight, you'll shut your fucking mouth right now," Jared said without looking back at her.

And, just like that, Crystal withdrew from the confrontation and abandoned her brother—*again.* She valued crack more than her family. Cody turned around to face Jared. He drew the baseball bat over his shoulder, as if he were about to swing it at him. To his dismay, Jared stood his ground. The drug dealer aimed the handgun at Cody's chest. Crystal breathed deeply as an air of tension smothered the room.

Jared said, "If you can't do it, then we can't trust you. You're just dead weight. We're better off killing you now, right?"

Teary-eyed, Cody glanced over at his sister. Crystal crossed her arms and looked away, ashamed. Cody was pushed into a corner at gunpoint. He believed Jared would really shoot him if he didn't cooperate. He looked at Mike. *No one's going to give a shit,* he told himself. He tapped Mike's forehead with the baseball bat—once, twice, and then a third time. Then he raised the bat over his head. His breathing accelerated and he felt the blood pumping through his veins.

He gasped, then he swung the baseball bat down at Mike's head. At the last second, Jared laughed and pulled him away. The bat missed Mike by a *centimeter,* nearly scraping his temple.

"Okay, psycho, calm down," Jared said, still chuckling. "Why didn't you tell me your balls dropped already? You're not as pussy as I thought, kid."

"Are you joking? I could have killed him! I almost–"

Jared slapped his hand over Cody's mouth. He said, "Stop screaming. You don't want to wake him up, do you? Then you'd really have to kill him."

Cody exhaled loudly through his nose. He pulled away from him, then he pushed the baseball bat against Jared's chest. Jared handed it to Crystal. He took the pocket-knife out of his backpack. He unfolded it, revealing a partially serrated three-and-a-half-inch blade. He knelt on the edge of the bed. He held the knife over Mike's belly button.

Cody asked, "What the hell are you doing?"

"Tomorrow night, you're going to knock on their door. When they answer, you're going to stab them."

"Wha–What?"

"It doesn't matter who answers the door," Jared continued. "It could be papa bear, mama bear, or one of the cubs. It does *not* matter. You need to show them we mean business, but I know you don't want to kill anyone, so I'm going to teach you a little lesson."

He tapped the tip of the blade against Mike's belly button, then he slid it down to his groin. He looked at Cody.

Jared said, "Stab them anywhere from there to here. There are no, um… 'vital' organs in this area.

You know, liver, kidneys, and all that shit. You'll cut into their guts, but they'll survive. When you stab them, you have to *really* get in there. Think of it like... like you're punching someone you hate with a knife." He grinned and said, "Like your dad. Yeah, just imagine you're stabbing your dad."

"I–I don't want to stab anyone."

"That's too bad 'cause, one way or another, you're doing it."

"Come on, man, *please.* I don't want to hurt anyone. It–It's not me. Why can't you do it?"

Jared responded, "While you're distracting them at the front door, I'm going to break into the house through the back with the gun. We're going to corner them, you understand? I don't have time to teach you how to shoot if things go wrong, so you have to use the knife. It's the only way."

Cody glanced over at his sister, panic in his eyes, and he asked, "Then why can't Crystal do it?"

Crystal sniffled and said, "I'm sorry, Cody. I have to wait in the car just in case one of you fucks up or those assholes fight back before we trap them. You can't drive, so you can't be the getaway driver."

"I–I can try to–to... I can do something. I can just, um... Maybe I can keep–"

"Cody, relax," Jared said in a calm, understanding tone.

For the first time since he met him, Cody felt a sense of security around Jared. There was something about his perpetual nonchalance that made him feel safe. *Everything's under control,* he thought, *I can't panic, not like this.* He drew a deep breath and stepped away from the bed.

Jared said, "Listen, kid, as long as you remember what I told you, everything will be fine. Get them talking, tell 'em you're trick r' treating, then stab them three times. Force yourself into the house and... that's it. You can stand in the corner with the bat for the rest of the night. We'll be out of there in less than two hours. After we leave, they'll go to a hospital, they'll file some reports, and then everything will go back to normal. It's that simple. Don't make this complicated, okay?"

"O–Okay..."

"So where are you going to stab them?"

"Un–Under the belly button."

"That's right. Then what?"

"Then... Then I go into the house and stand in the corner."

Jared closed the pocket-knife and said, "Looks like we've got ourselves the perfect plan." As he walked out of the room, he said, "Let's go to the party store before it closes. We need costumes."

Crystal stumbled out of the room as she tripped over a garbage bag. She followed her boyfriend out of the apartment, begging for a hit of crack every step of the way. Cody stayed behind. He watched the unconscious drug dealer while contemplating the meaning of life. *How the hell did we end up here?*–he asked himself. He was surrounded by desperation and violence. The Cohens offered them an escape route.

But at what cost?

He joined Crystal and Jared at the muscle car in the parking lot. They went to a local party store. They purchased a roll of duct tape, a Halloween makeup kit, and some cheap costumes.

Chapter Six

Halloween

Dustin sat on his bed and read the last text message he sent to Natalie. The message to his girlfriend read: *I'm going to be a little late to the party. Sorry, Nat.* It was followed by a frowning emoji and a broken heart emoji. He sent the message seven minutes ago. He was dressed and ready to go volunteer, but he needed to hear from Natalie first.

"Come on, come on," he murmured.

The phone buzzed. He received a message from Natalie. The message read: *Lol it's okay, I was probably going to be late anyway.* A second message, sent immediately after the first, read: *Just text me when you're ready to meet.* That message was followed by a kissing emoji and two heart emojis. She wasn't a strict, obnoxious girlfriend.

Dustin smiled and whispered, "That's why I love you."

He grabbed his car keys, then he exited his bedroom. He stopped before reaching the end of the hall. He peeked into Jill's bedroom. His sister sat on a chair in front of a vanity table. She painted her face white with water-based makeup. She was in the process of designing a skull on her face. It was a simple but timeless costume.

Dustin leaned on the doorway and asked, "So, you're heading out to the party?"

Jill looked at him through the reflection on the mirror. She said, "Yup."

"I thought you'd be busy studying. You skipped last year's party, didn't you?"

"I had to keep my grades up last year. I'm doing fine this year. Finished all my tests, got my recommendations and references, and filled out my paperwork. I'm ready for everything and anything. Now I just have to party."

"Well, *congratulations,*" Dustin said with a hint of sarcasm in his voice. He was simultaneously proud and jealous of her. He said, "Seriously, though, don't go around hooking up with any guys at the party. You know they all want one thing."

Jill huffed, then she said, "You know I'm not like that."

"I know, I'm just saying," Dustin said. He took a step away from the door, then he stepped back and leaned into the room. He said, "And don't drink *anything*. Like, nothing at all, okay? Some douchebags like to spike the drinks at these sorts of things."

Jill turned around and said, "Oh my God, Dustin, you *know* I'm not like that."

Dustin snickered, then he said, "Good girl..."

"Good girl," Jill repeated mockingly. She turned around and continued painting her face. She smiled and whispered, "Such a dork..."

The siblings didn't have the best relationship. They were competitive, they often annoyed each other, but they cared about one another.

Dustin entered the living room. He found his father watching *The Exorcist* on TV, a bowl of popcorn on his lap and a glass full of Coca-Cola and ice on the side table. He was dressed as Sheriff Woody from *Toy Story.* He was only missing the cowboy hat and the boots. The cheap vest, dappled with cow spots, helped him resemble the character. Otherwise, he looked like a guy in a yellow shirt.

Dustin saw his mother and his other sister in the kitchen over the bar. They spent quality time decorating some cookies.

Shannon was already dressed and ready for the night. She complemented her husband's costume by dressing as Bo Peep from *Toy Story 4.* She wore a blue jumpsuit, a headband, an arm band, a wrist band, and a cape. Her staff was somewhere in her bedroom. Kimberly wasn't ready. She wore a white dress with a red trim. She was supposed to be the Annabelle doll from the *Conjuring* universe of movies. She only needed to apply the doll makeup.

Upon noticing him, Shannon said, "Hey, baby, you coming trick r' treating with us?"

Dustin said, "Can't. I'm going to volunteer at the shelter, then I'm going to the big party."

"You're volunteering? *Today?*"

"Yeah, that's, um… That's what I said."

Eyes on the movie, Patrick said, "We talked about this, hun. He's not a teenager anymore. He needs to build character and work on that résumé."

"But it's Halloween, Pat, and it's almost four," Shannon said as she made her way to the living room. She stood beside her son, hands on her hips. She asked, "Couldn't he have done it tomorrow or the day after? He should be spending time with the family, remember? Maybe passing out candy or trick r' treating with us."

"He's not complaining, is he? It's good for him, hun. Besides, the sooner he heads out, the sooner he can come back. That's that."

Shannon rolled her eyes. She adjusted her son's coat, then she kissed his cheek. They didn't have to say a word to communicate. Their eyes said the same thing: *the old man is a stubborn guy.* They headed to the front door. Shannon glanced over her shoulder. Kimberly joined her father in the living room, munching on popcorn while enjoying the movie.

Shannon whispered, "You can leave early. Trust me, they won't mind at the shelter. Come back by seven, get dressed, and then maybe we can go trick r' treating before you head out with that cute Natalie girl. *Or* you can bring her over and I can finally meet her."

"I don't know about that last part mom, but I'll definitely try to get back early," Dustin said, smirking.

"Okay, okay. Be safe, baby. I love you."

"Love you, too. See you in a few!"

Chapter Seven

Trick R' Treat

Patrick grabbed a cookie from the plate on the kitchen bar. The cookie was designed to resemble a 'Good Guys' doll from *Child's Play.* It wasn't an exact replica, but the orange icing at the top gave it away. He took a bite. Crumbs fell onto his shirt and down to the counter. He licked the icing off his lips, then he took another bite.

"Well, what do you think?" Kimberly asked. "They're garbage, aren't they? We should just throw them away. Everyone's going to think I'm trying to poison them."

With his mouth full of cookie crumbs and icing, Patrick said, "Wait... they're... delicious. I just..." He swallowed loudly, then he said, "I need a glass of milk."

"They're dry? And they're hard, too, right? I knew it."

"They're fine, baby. I'm just saying: every cookie tastes better with milk. It's a scientific fact."

"I guess that's true..."

"Of course it is! Have you ever–"

The doorbell echoed through the house.

Patrick nudged his daughter's arm with his elbow and said, "Looks like the babies are out trick r' treating already. You wanna come pass out some candy with me?"

"In a minute," Kimberly responded as she focused on her cookies. She grabbed a piping bag filled with red icing and said, "I think I can fix this one's hair."

"Good luck, kiddo."

Patrick went to the front door. He grabbed a bowl of candy from the console table in the entrance hall. He gave it a shake to mix the candy, then he opened the door. The sky was painted with every tint of orange, blue, purple, and black as the sun fell. Three kids in costumes piled into the backseat of an SUV next door, babbling and giggling. Their parents followed them, tripping over their capes. The family was heading to *Oro Center* for the big party.

Otherwise, the end of the cul-de-sac was empty.

"A little early to be trick r' treating, isn't it?" Patrick asked. He furrowed his brow as he examined his visitor. He said, "And you're a little old to be trick r' treating alone... right now... at... What time is it? Five-forty-five? You are trick r' treating, aren't you?"

Cody stood on the porch—hood up, head down. He wore a hockey mask splattered with fake blood. He held the open pocket-knife in his pocket, the blade tearing through the twill. He looked back at the street upon hearing the SUV's purring engine. He watched as they made a U-turn and drove *away* from the house at the dead-end.

Now or never, he told himself. Yet, he could barely hear his inner voice due to his loud, panicked breathing.

Patrick grabbed a handful of candy from the bowl and asked, "So, are you carrying it all in your pockets? Or do you need a bag? We've got a few reusable shopping bags in the kitchen if you want." He glanced back into his home and shouted, "Shannon! Kimberly! Can you bring one of those bags from under the–"

Cody pulled his hands out of his pockets. He grabbed Patrick's yellow button-up shirt with his left hand and pressed his forehead against his chest. Then he thrust the knife into him. Adrenaline pumping through his veins and fear of failure infecting his mind, he lost complete control of himself. He stabbed him three times, as planned, then four, and then five, and then *six times.*

Patrick didn't realize he was being attacked until the third stab. First, Cody stabbed the left side of his lower abdomen. The blade tore through his jeans and flesh, then cracked his hip bone. Then he thrust the blade through the left side of his abdomen, as if he were hitting him with a hook. The blade sliced his large intestine. With the third stab, he drove the blade through his belly button.

Upon realizing he was being stabbed, Patrick instinctively covered the wounds on his stomach with his hands. And he regretted it.

Cody stabbed his left hand. The short blade impaled his hand, entering through the back of his hand and exiting through his palm. The center bones of his palm—the third and fourth metacarpals—were shattered. The blade slid out with a moist *crunching* sound. For the fifth stab, the blade cut into his forearm. As he pulled it out, the wound stretched and widened.

His forearm, along with his sleeve, was torn open, exposing his fibrous muscle and blue veins. The sleeve of his shirt was soaked in blood within seconds. The blood dripped from the bush of hair on his arm, too.

With the final stab, Cody thrust the blade at Patrick's pubic region. He missed his penis by *two* inches. Patrick felt the hot blood cascading over his genitals. It was a terrifying sensation. His dick shriveled up and hid in his bloody pubic hair.

Patrick pushed the blade out of him and staggered back—shirt, jeans, and hands drenched in blood. He breathed shallowly, shocked by the attack. His lips shook, but he couldn't say anything. He looked at his attacker—a masked teenager—then he lowered his head and watched as his blood rained down onto the hardwood floor. The crotch of his jeans looked dark, as if he had pissed himself.

He stammered, "Wha–Wha–What did–did you–"

Shannon shrieked in the living room.

Kimberly cried, "Daddy!"

Lightheaded, Patrick stumbled down the hall. His glasses fell off his face as he crashed into a wall. He stepped on his glasses without noticing.

He mumbled, "Wha–What's happening?"

Cody looked down at himself in awe. Patrick's blood landed on him, but it wasn't visible against his black clothing. The red beads of blood clung to his leather gloves, like sweat on a sprinter's brow. He entered the house. He closed the door behind him, then he peeked through the peephole. The cul-de-sac was empty.

Patrick's eyes widened and he fell to his knees. In the living room, Jared stood between the end of the dining table and the sliding patio doors. His face was painted to resemble a clown's—a white face, black around the eyes, and a wide, red smile that stretched across his cheeks. He forced Kimberly to stand in front of him. He placed the muzzle of his pistol against her temple. Tears flowed down the girl's rosy face as she sobbed uncontrollably.

Her arms in front of her, Shannon cried, "Please don't hurt my baby! *Please!*"

"Be quiet," Jared said. "All of you, be quiet."

"Let her go," Patrick said as he crawled towards the dining table. He tried to stand up, but he tripped over himself and hit the floor again. He said, "Don't hurt her, you little punk."

Jill jogged into the living room, baffled by the ruckus. She slid to a stop beside her mother. She saw Cody to her left, a bloody knife in his hand, and Jared to her right, holding her little sister hostage. Her instincts told her to run—*to get help.* She lurched down the hall to grab her cell phone.

Before she could reach her room, Jared shouted, "Everyone, shut up!" He tapped Kimberly's head with the barrel of the gun and barked, "Get back here! If you're not here in five seconds, I'm going to blow this little bitch's brains out! Five!"

Shannon fell to her knees, clasped her hands in front of her chest, and begged, "Please! Don't do it! Oh my God, don't do it!"

"Four!"

Patrick struggled to his feet and said, "Baby, it's okay."

"I don't wanna die," Kimberly squeaked out, her voice cracking.

"Three!" Jared shouted as he took a step back with his hostage so Patrick wouldn't tackle them. "Two!"

Jill rushed back into the living room, her hands over her head. Her makeup was smeared by her tears.

Her mind was flooded with hopes and regrets: *I hope we won't die, I should have called the cops as soon as I heard the screaming, I hope Dustin's okay, I should have just ran to get help.*

She stuttered, "O–Okay, pl–please don't hurt her." She swallowed loudly and locked eyes with her crying sister. Her lips twitched as she tried to smile. She said, "I'm sorry, kiddo."

Kimberly repeated, "I don't wanna die."

Patrick leaned over one of the dining chairs and asked, "What do you... want from us?"

Jared said, "I want you all to sit down on that couch and listen to my deal. If you listen, if you cooperate, then no one else will get hurt." He shrugged at Patrick and said, "Sorry about the stabbing, man. We just needed you to know that we meant business. But you'll make it out of this as long as you follow our directions. Got it? Can we all just sit down now?"

Patrick glanced around the living room. Shannon, Jill, and Kimberly sniveled. They were terrified but they were unharmed. He was stabbed multiple times, but he knew he could survive for a few more hours without medical assistance. The stabbing was sloppy, but it wasn't a lethal attack. He looked back at Cody. Through the holes on his mask, he saw the fear in the teenager's eyes. He guessed it was his first time robbing a family and he wasn't trying to kill him.

He said, "I'm... I'm going to need my first-aid kit."

Jared responded, "We can talk about it after we make our deal. Until then, you're free to patch yourself up on the couch. Put some pressure on those cuts, tie yourself off... That sort of thing."

"Yeah, yeah, I get it... Can you, um... Can you get

that gun away from my daughter's head? It's making me real anxious."

"As soon as you sit down."

"Okay, okay," Patrick said. He nodded at Kimberly and said, "Everything's fine, sweetie. Just follow their directions. Okay?"

Kimberly couldn't respond. She wanted to repeat herself again: *I don't wanna die.* Patrick sat down on the sofa while keeping his eyes on Jared. He leaned over the armrest and examined the damage on his forearm. His forearm was split open horizontally. He cut the sleeve off his shirt, then he tied it around his forearm to try to seal the wound and slow the bleeding. Shannon sat down beside him, moving with reluctance. She took off her cape and pressed it against the wounds on her husband's lower abdomen. She kept glancing back at her youngest daughter. Jill joined them. She sat with her hands up, frozen in place. Her face was paler than the remaining white makeup caked on her skin.

"Sit," Jared demanded as he pushed Kimberly towards the recliner.

Kimberly sat down on her father's favorite seat, shivering and whimpering.

Patrick said, "Can she sit with–"

"Shut up," Jared interrupted. He sat on the coffee table across from the family while pointing the pistol at Shannon. Without taking his eyes off them, he said, "Alright, we're settled here. Go get her."

"Wha–What?" Shannon stuttered.

"I wasn't talking to you. Sit quietly and don't move."

Cody wiped his hands on his black hoodie as he

ran out of the house. He slipped on the puddle of blood on the porch, but he quickly regained his balance. Crouched down, he jogged past the neighbor's house and then another's. To his relief, the end of the cul-de-sac was calm. A few houses down, however, neighbors were preparing for the trick r' treaters.

"Just a little more time," he whispered. He reached the muscle car parked behind a dumpster. He knocked on the passenger window and said, "Come on, come on."

Crystal sat in the driver's seat, dozing in and out of consciousness. It had been almost a day since she last smoked any crack. She wore an orange wig. Some fake blood was painted onto her forehead and chin. Although she understood the risks, she was too annoyed to properly disguise herself, like Jared and her brother. She waited in the car as the getaway driver.

She rolled the window down and asked, "What's up? Are we good?"

"We're good. Let's go already."

Crystal rolled the window up. She grabbed the backpack from the backseat and hopped out of the car. The siblings jogged back to the Cohen house just as dusk arrived. Crystal taped a sign onto the front door. The sign read: *No candy, sorry! Do not disturb!* They entered the house and locked the door behind them. The porch light went out, leaving the house and its inhabitants in a void of darkness and despair.

Chapter Eight

The Finer Details

"So, now that we're all here, let me tell you how this is going to go down," Jared said.

The Cohens remained seated. Patrick was covered in a layer of cold sweat while blood pooled around his lower abdomen. Shannon whispered words of comfort into his ear while trying to stay calm. Jill kept her hands up, staring vacantly at the floor. Kimberly continued sobbing, digging her fingernails into the armrests.

Cody and Crystal stood behind the sofa. Cody was now armed with a baseball bat and Crystal held a machete in her hand. The blinds and curtains were closed. The lights were turned off in every room, except the living room and kitchen.

Jared said, "First of all, we are *robbing* you. We don't want to *hurt* you, we don't want to *kill* you, we only want to rob you. It's important that you understand that 'cause I don't want you to do something stupid out of fear. Like I said, you'll live if you don't give us a hard time. Hell, maybe you can even make it to the big party. Okay?"

Patrick said, "Take whatever you want and leave."

"We will. We're going to go through every room in this house and we're going to take *everything* that's worth a damn. But we want more."

"What else... What else can we give you?"

"Money. Lots and lots of money."

Shannon stuttered, "I–I have some cash in my

purse."

Jared chuckled, then he said, "We're not looking for chump change, ma'am, but we'll take that. No, we're looking for the 'big catch.' You get me? So, my lady friend here is going to escort you to your local bank. You're going to go to the clerk and you're going to withdraw nine-thousand-five-hundred dollars. They shouldn't ask since it isn't over ten grand, but, if they do, you tell 'em it's for a car. 'I'm buying my daughter a used car and I want to pay in cash.' You hear me? Repeat it."

Shannon swallowed loudly, then she said, "I'm buying my daughter a–a used car and I want to pay in cash."

"Good. Real good. But try not to stutter. We don't want them to get suspicious. You wanna know why?"

Shannon shook her head, then she nodded. She was confused, concerned, nervous, and terrified.

Jared explained, "If you tell the clerk about this—if you tell *anyone* about this—and the cops somehow get involved, my lady friend will tell me. Then everyone dies."

"Oh God," Shannon said, tears trickling from her eyes as she blinked.

Patrick said, "Please, guys, let's not do anything rash."

Jill cried, "We didn't do anything wrong."

Kimberly covered her face with her hands and sobbed. Their voices overlapped as they begged for mercy. Crystal tightened her grip on the machete and rubbed her temple. The noise was irritating. Cody saw pure, unadulterated fear. It reminded him of the first time his father beat his sister with a wire hanger—the screaming, the tears, the pain, *the blood.*

Speaking loudly but not shouting, Jared said, "You see, *this...* this isn't going to work. So, it's time to take some precautionary measures." He beckoned to Kimberly and said, "Get up, girl."

Patrick leaned forward and barked, "Don't you touch her!"

"If you get up from that seat, I'm going to cave this girl's skull in. Do you understand me?"

"You little bastard. You're going straight to–"

"*Do you* understand me, motherfucker?"

Patrick wanted to fight back, but he was debilitated by the stabbing. One punch to the gut would have paralyzed him. He couldn't dodge bullets, either. He sank back into his seat, gritting his teeth.

Shannon asked, "What are you going to do to my baby?"

"I'm not going to hurt her," Jared said. "I'm going to keep her quiet and I'm going to help her stay still. You should be thanking me for this. She won't get herself killed by doing something stupid now."

He dragged Kimberly to the corner of the room. She tried to pull away, but she wasn't strong enough. He forced her to sit down on the floor, wedged between the wall and a console table. He grabbed the duct tape from his bag. He taped her ankles and wrists together ten times over. Then he placed a strip of duct tape over her mouth.

He whispered, "Don't move, baby."

Kimberly wanted to say something along the lines of: *get away from me, you creep!* But her voice was muffled.

Jared pointed at Jill and said, "Your turn. Come on,

hurry up. The faster we get this done, the faster your dad can get to a hospital."

Jill stared at her parents as she stood up slowly. Her parents looked back at her, helpless. She yelped as Jared grabbed her arm and dragged her to the corner. He forced her to sit beside her little sister, then he repeated the process: he taped her wrists, her ankles, and her mouth.

"Peace and quiet," Crystal murmured.

Jared returned to his seat on the coffee table. He said, "Now that that's settled, let me ask you two a question. Does anyone else live here? Hmm? Are you expecting company tonight? Anything like that?"

Dustin—the parents thought about their son. Patrick was relieved. He sent Dustin to volunteer until eight o'clock, so he assumed he wouldn't get home until eight-thirty or eight-forty-five. By then, he hoped the robbery would be over. Shannon was horrified. She gave Dustin permission to leave early. If he arrived during the robbery, everything could go downhill in the blink of an eye.

Before Shannon could say a word, Patrick said, "We're all here. We're not expecting anyone."

Don't come home, Shannon prayed. *Please, Dustin, go straight to the party. Don't come to this living nightmare. Save yourself, honey.*

Patrick continued, "Listen, pal... Why don't you just take the stuff in the safe? In the master bedroom's closet, there's a... a safe in there."

"What's in it?"

"My jewelry," Shannon said. "You can sell it for thousands. Take it all."

Jared smiled and said, "I'll take it right after you

two leave. I need a phone."

"There's one in my purse. Can I... Can I grab it? It's right there on the counter."

"No, not now. You'll need yours in a minute. *You*, sir. Give me your phone."

Patrick smiled thinly and shook his head, clearly frustrated. He said, "It's in my right pocket. It's probably... busted because of the blood."

Jared said, "Bash his head in if he tries anything stupid." Cody stood as still as a mannequin. Jared said, "Get ready, retard."

Cody snapped out of his contemplation. He held the baseball bat in both hands and tapped the back of Patrick's head with it. Patrick sneered at him, then he hissed in pain. Jared reached into Patrick's left pocket, his eyes glued to the man's. He pulled the cell phone out of his pocket. It was moist, but it wasn't damaged by the blood. He wiped it with his shirt, then he swiped his finger across the screen.

He asked, "What's your pin?" Patrick muttered indistinctly. Jared said, "Stop wasting my damn time. Do you want to die here? Huh? Do you want me to hurt your girls? Tell me your pin so we can finish this already. Stop fucking around."

"It's nine-three-six-six, damn it!"

Nine-three-six-six—the phone unlocked.

As he swiped through his contacts, Jared asked, "And what's your name, ma'am?"

"Sha-Shannon."

Jared said, "Shannon... So you'd be under... 'Shan,' right? Shan with the little heart next to it?" He chuckled, then he said, "Cute. Real cute, guys. How old are you?"

Her lips shaking, Shannon asked, "Is that a serious question?"

"No, it's not. I don't give a shit. Now go answer your phone."

"My phone?"

♪ *Don't tell me that it's over! 'Cause I know it ain't over!*

Shannon's ringtone went off in the kitchen—the chorus of Kimberly's favorite song. She looked at her daughters, then at her husband, and then at Jared. She was the only healthy, unrestrained member of the family, but she couldn't do a thing to save them. She couldn't overpower three armed intruders after all.

"Everything's okay, everything's okay," she said.

She trudged to the kitchen. She took her cell phone out of her bag. For a second, she thought about grabbing a knife from the knife block. Instead, she answered the call and returned to the living room.

She asked, "What do you want me to do?"

Jared said, "You're leaving. You're going to the bank."

"Let me go," Patrick said. "I have access to all of our accounts and I'm a much better actor than her."

Jared said, "Acting can't wipe away all that blood. Now sit there and be quiet." He turned his attention to Shannon and said, "Hand your phone over to my lady friend there. We're going to stay connected *every* step of the way. If the call disconnects or if she tells me about any trouble, someone's going to get hurt. You'll also be able to hear us here if you cooperate, so you'll know your family is safe. When you come back with the cash, we'll take all of your phones and leave.

As soon as we're out of your sight, you can run to a neighbor and call for help. Easy, right? Yeah, that's right. Now go. The clock is ticking."

Shannon handed her phone to Crystal. Crystal handed the machete to Cody. She needed a discreet weapon, so she took the pocket-knife from her brother.

As she reluctantly followed her captor to the front door, Shannon looked at her family and said, "I love you. I love all of you so much. Everything will be okay. You hear me, babies? I'll be back!"

"Be careful!" Patrick shouted from the sofa. "And don't you touch her!"

The Cohen sisters cried in the corner of the room while huddling close together. The ongoing robbery traumatized them. Kimberly loved horror movies, but she never experienced *true* dread until that evening. Jill was always a gentle, squeamish girl, so she was terrified from the beginning. She could only hope her mother would be okay.

As the front door closed, Jared nodded at Cody and said, "Go lock it." While Cody went to the door, Jared looked at Patrick and said, "Let's see what you've got in this little palace of yours."

Chapter Nine

Acquainted

"Kid. Hey, kid," Patrick whispered. "You don't have to do this. You can walk away with your dignity. I know you're just a-a troubled kid in a bad situation. I forgive you and I can convince any prosecutor, jury, or judge in this state to forgive you, too. I have friends, *connections.* You'll get a slap on the wrist, a clear conscience, and a second chance. Help us out, kid."

Cody stood behind the sofa. He gripped the machete in his right hand and aimed it at the man's head. In his other hand, he held Patrick's cell phone up to his ear and listened to his sister and her hostage. He heard a few insignificant words and the *purr* of the SUV's engine over the phone. Yet, he felt as if he were listening to a dozen shouting voices at once while a monster roared in the background.

He squeezed his eyes shut and shook his head, as if he could throw the voices out of his skull through his ears. He tapped the back of Patrick's head with the machete.

He said, "Just stay quiet. It's almost over."

"You can end this now, kid."

"*Shut. Up.* You don't want to make him angry."

Patrick furrowed his brow. He wondered if the teenager was nervous about committing his first robbery or if he feared his partner more than anything else. The Cohen sisters continued sobbing in the corner. They communicated through their eyes, promising to stick together until the end.

Jared walked around the kitchen. He stopped in front of the fridge—a smart refrigerator with a touchscreen panel. A slideshow of the family's last vacation in Hawaii played on the screen. He noticed a young man in some of the pictures—*Dustin Cohen.* He opened the fridge and peeked inside. He found fresh meats and vegetables, soy and almond milk, an assortment of fruit juices, eggs, bacon, and more.

And all of the groceries were neatly organized.

"The perfect family," he whispered.

He ate one of Kimberly's cookies. It was decorated to resemble *Pennywise the Dancing Clown.* He dumped a short stream of soy milk into his mouth, avoiding direct contact so he wouldn't leave any damning evidence behind. He grimaced in disgust. He drank some of the almond milk. He grimaced again.

He shouted, "Don't you have any normal food around this place?!"

Patrick sighed, then he muttered, "Psycho..."

Jared returned to the living room. He crouched in front of the Cohen sisters. He tapped his temple with the barrel of the pistol while running his eyes over them. Jill wore a camisole and pajama shorts. Since she sat with her knees up to her face, her ass and part of her underwear were visible. Kimberly wore her costume—the *Annabelle* dress. He ran his eyes from her toes to her shins, then he glared at her crotch, as if he were trying to shoot lasers from his eyes to burn through her clothing.

He asked, "You girls want to get acquainted?"

The sisters shook their heads and whimpered.

Patrick said, "Stay away from them."

Jared continued, "We're going to be here for a

while. If you can promise me that you'll behave, I might be able to take that tape off you."

"Don't listen to him."

"We can talk. We can eat and drink. We can, um... How do I say it? We can exchange favors. Yeah, you scratch my back, I'll scratch yours. You interested?"

"Leave them alone!" Patrick barked.

Ignoring him, Jared asked, "What do you say, ladies?"

Again, the sisters shook their heads. Rivers of tears and blobs of mucus rolled over the duct tape on their mouths. Jared pushed his tongue against the side of his mouth and nodded, trying to bottle his frustration. Cody didn't understand any of it. They planned and rehearsed everything, but Jared ignored the script.

Patrick said, "They're good girls. We're good people. You... You're a monster. I can tell *you* planned all of this. Yeah, you... you little, selfish, cowardly punk."

"Shut up," Jared said.

"Oh, fuck you. Stabbing me, tormenting my innocent girls, sending my wife away... Who do you think you are? Huh? You think you're some... some robber in a comic book? Some supervillain or something? You're not. You're a *coward,* kid. You hear me? A *cow*-ard."

Jared approached the sofa. He bent over, hands on his knees, and he gazed into Patrick's teary, bloodshot eyes. He couldn't help but snicker. He saw *him* as the true coward, not the other way around.

"Who do I think I am?" he said. "No. Who do *you* think you are? You think you're the hero of this story?

Is that it? You're going to save everyone, get your picture on Twitter and go viral, meet the President and get a medal? That's not how it's going to go down, man. Look at yourself. My boy here cut you a few times and you're... you're done already. You wouldn't be able to beat *his* ass and he's pure pussy. Do you really think you can beat mine?"

"I–I'm not a–afraid of you."

"Would you be afraid of me if I shot your daughter?"

"You wouldn't."

Jared stepped back. He aimed the pistol at the girls. The sisters flinched and cried while moving closer together.

Cody asked, "What are you doing?"

"Don't!" Patrick shouted.

Jared asked, "Which one should I shoot? The young one? The older one? Both? Which one's your favorite?"

"Okay! I get it! You're the boss! You're a big fucking man, alright?!"

"I didn't ask you that," Jared said as he crouched down beside the girls. He placed the pistol against Kimberly's head, causing her to howl and shake. He asked, "The kid? Should I shoot the kid?"

"Don't do it! Please! You–You have your whole life ahead of you! Don't do it!"

"You're not answering me, man! I'll give you five seconds, then I'll shoot them both!"

Patrick leaned forward, but Cody pressed the blade against his neck and grabbed his shoulder with his other hand before he could fall off the sofa. Crystal could hear the ruckus over the phone, but she was nodding off in the SUV. To Shannon, it looked like nothing was happening at her home.

Patrick shouted, "Shit! Let me go!"

"He won't do it," Cody cried. "Just sit down and shut up, man!"

Jared said, "Five, four, three…"

"You little punk!" Patrick hissed.

"Two… One…"

Patrick yelled, "Don't shoot my Kimmy! Don't shoot the little one! Don't shoot her… please, don't shoot her…" Out of breath, he looked at Jill and said, "I'm sorry, baby. I'm so sorry."

Jared aimed the gun at Jill's head. Jill fell back against the wall and cried hysterically. Her words were muffled, but they understood her. Victims of murder shared the same vocabulary before dying: *don't kill me, I don't want to die, please, no, no, no, no, no!* She felt her heart pounding against her chest, as if it were about to burst out like an alien in a horror movie. She thought about her family and friends, her future and past, her life and death.

Jared chuckled, then he said, "I guess I'm not the coward after all." He pointed the gun at Kimberly and said, "And I guess you're the favorite. Your daddy really loves you, baby. I hope I don't have to hurt you tonight."

"You little bastard," Patrick cried. "You're crazy. You're a monster. Those are girls. They're innocent."

"But you're not. And you're getting on my nerves. I need to teach you a lesson."

"Just take the jewelry and leave!"

"I will… in a minute."

Jared grabbed a lamp from a console table. He

disconnected it from the wall. He used a boxcutter to cut the cord, then he returned the lamp to the table. He gave Cody a gentle shove.

Cody stuttered, "Wha–What are you going to do?"

Before Patrick could look over his shoulder, Jared wrapped the thick, durable cord around his neck and pulled back. He used it as a garotte.

"What the hell?" Patrick croaked out as he scratched at the cable.

The fear of suffocation caused him to panic. He reached for his neck, staining his skin with the blood on his hands. The blood, along with his cold sweat, made it difficult for him to get a grip on the cord. His fingers slid off it and his fingernails tore into his neck. Two thin lacerations turned into three, then four, then five, and then six. The cuts stung. Droplets of blood leaked out of the wounds and blended with the rest of it.

He kicked at the floorboards and jerked left-and-right, but he couldn't escape Jared's grip. His vision blurred and his hearing faded. His daughters were a blot in his vision and their voices were slow and distorted. He was struck by a pounding headache. His head was heavy, as if it were being flooded with blood. He believed his head was going to explode. Saliva foamed out of his mouth. His arms became limp, but his legs continued to shake.

Cody said, "You're killing him..."

Jared kept tugging on the cord.

Although her voice was muffled, Jill crawled forward and shouted the same: *You're killing him!*

After forty-five seconds, Jared loosened his grip on the cord. Patrick's head fell forward. A string of drool hung out of his mouth. He drew short, raspy breaths while his head spun.

Jared leaned close to his ear and asked, "What's the combination to your safe? The one you said you had in your bedroom?"

Patrick didn't respond. He coughed as he rubbed his red, bloody neck. A jolt of pain surged from his throat with each swallow.

Jared asked, "What's the combination?"

Patrick couldn't say a word. Jared tugged on the cord again, pulling Patrick back against the backrest of the sofa.

"Wa–Wait," Patrick said in a hoarse tone.

Jared gritted his teeth as he pulled on the cord. He counted to fifteen, then he loosened his grip. He gave Patrick five seconds to catch his breath, then he tugged on the cord again. He stared at Patrick's crotch while doing so. *Autoerotic asphyxiation*—he always thought of it as a rich man's sport, so he wanted to see if the strangulation would arouse him.

It didn't.

He released the cord after another fifteen seconds. Then he repeated the process: strangle, breathe, strangle, breathe, *strangle.* Patrick's face went from blood-red to pale while his neck turned blue and red—bruised and swollen. He was barely conscious. His daughters begged Jared to stop, but they didn't dare move away from that corner. And Cody watched from the sidelines, horrified.

Jared asked, "Have you had enough? Do you respect me yet, motherfucker?!" Patrick nodded as a squelching sound came out of his mouth. Jared released his grip on the cord and asked, "So what's the combination?"

Patrick wheezed. The whistle of each breath was louder than his daughters' sobbing. He rubbed his neck and leaned against the armrest. During the strangulation, he forgot about the stab wounds across his lower abdomen. He was bleeding again. The blood soaked the seat under him. He sounded like a completely different man. His once soothing voice was now hoarse, as if phlegm were obstructing his throat.

"It's... It's... a... pin," he said weakly. "Nine... One... Seven... Th–Three... Five... Zero..."

"Ninety-one, seventy-three, fifty. Is that right?"

Patrick could only nod.

"Good, I'll get to that soon," Jared said.

He strolled back to the coffee table and took a seat. The girls moved back to the corner and cowered. They felt useless during the violent confrontation.

Jared said, "Sorry about that. I've got a bad temper. A *very* bad temper." He chuckled and swiped his fingers through his hair. Some of the makeup on his brow was smudged by his sweat. He said, "I want to tell you something. Can you hear me okay? Do you need a minute? We've got plenty of time."

"I can... I can hear you," Patrick responded. "Don't... hurt... them."

"I'm not going to hurt them. Not now, at least."

"Oh God, why?" Patrick cried.

"I want to tell you about my trip to Mexico. Have you ever been to Mexico?"

Patrick mumbled the same thing over and over: *oh God, oh God, oh God.* He was suffering from excruciating physical and emotional pain.

Jared continued, "I'm a drug dealer, you know? Weed, crack, heroin, PCP, ecstasy, I'll sell anything. I'd sell it to your wife or little daughter right here and I wouldn't bat an eyelash. A few years ago, I used to think I was the baddest motherfucker out there. I was getting into fights every day, stabbing people on the weekends, and I even shot at a few people when I lived in Vegas. I don't usually admit this 'cause I feel like the cops are always listening, but... You see that crowbar in that bag right there? I've had that for years. Two years ago, I went to a buddy's house. You don't have to know which city or state or country, but... you only have to know that he pissed me off. So, I caved his skull in with that crowbar. I beat him until his head was covered in blood, until his eyes popped out of his skull and then his brains came out of his eye sockets, until pieces of his skull were floating in his blood. It's true. It's so fucking true. I have a *very* bad temper, man."

He laughed maniacally and slapped his knees. Patrick was disgusted. He couldn't understand how a young man could gloat about killing a 'buddy.' The Cohen sisters heard everything, too. They were shocked by the descriptions of violence. Cody didn't know about *that* side of Jared's life. *He's a killer?*–he thought, the mask hiding the fear written on his face. He wasn't holding the machete up anymore. His arms dangled down to his sides.

Jared said, "But let me get to Mexico. You see, I went down there last year to secure a deal with some... 'potential business partners.' Yeah, let's call 'em that. I wanted to get my hands on more product so I can create a little empire here. Another buddy of mine took me on a little tour. I loved that place. Cheap women, cheap alcohol, cheap drugs... Paradise, you know?" He chuckled, reminiscent eyes staring into the past. With a steady face, he said, "Then I was taken to this room. They told me they caught a rival and they wanted me to check it out. They had this Mexican guy tied to a chair... and they tortured him. He was hit with, um... with batons, like the ones police use. He was coughing up blood. Then they cut one of his ears off, and then his tongue. That was painful to watch, man. You ever see someone get their tongue cut off? It's bloody. Bloodier than you are right now. Saliva makes it hard to get a good grip on a person's tongue. You start cutting into it, then you lose your grip, so then you start again. It's a long, bloody process... Anyway, then I heard the chainsaw. *Holy shit,* the chainsaw, man... They cut his hands off with it, then his feet, and then... You ever watch a beheading video, sir? Picture that, except I watched it live."

"S–Stop," Patrick said. "Jesus Christ, why are you... telling me this?"

"Because I want you to understand who you're fucking with. I couldn't make a deal out there in Mexico, but I learned a couple of things. This sort of shit... It's been a part of my life since I was born. I'm not afraid to hurt you and I *know* how to hurt you without killing you. I know how to hurt your daughters and your wife, too. *Torture,* sir, I know all about torture and murder. So, show a little respect. Stop interrupting me when I'm trying to chat with your girls, stop trying to get under my skin. You're just going to end up making things worse for everyone. Are we clear?"

"I... I understand."

"Good. Let me just make sure you *really* get where I'm coming from."

Jared went to the kitchen. He grabbed a stainless-steel chef's knife from a knife block, then he returned to the living room. He stopped in front of Patrick.

Upon spotting the sharp knife, Patrick grabbed Jared's forearm, but his grip was weak. Jared thrust the knife into Patrick's upper chest, avoiding his vital organs. Patrick's left clavicle broke with a loud *snap*. The man gasped and tightened his grip on Jared's arm. The knife *plopped* out, blood dripping from the blade.

The girls screamed: *No!*

Jared stabbed him again. He thrust the blade into the right side of his chest, but he missed his clavicle. So, he stabbed him a third time. He broke his right clavicle. Since he thrust the knife at him at an angle, the blade managed to rupture his bursa—the fluid-filled sac in his shoulder. His bone *crunched* as the blade was removed.

The stabbing was calculated. The broken clavicles caused shoulder pain with the slightest movement. The ruptured bursa damaged his entire right arm. Patrick felt the pain from his shoulder to his fingertips. He was already stabbed in the lower abdomen and his voice was damaged by the strangulation. He couldn't scream, he couldn't fight.

Between breaths, he asked, "Why are... you... doing this?"

Chapter Ten

The Talk

Crystal sat in the passenger seat of the SUV. She leaned against the door and held the phone up to her ear while keeping her eyes on Shannon, who sat in the driver's seat. She heard the chaos at the house—the crying, the screaming, *the begging*. She even heard the sounds of the stabbing. The *snap* of Patrick's clavicle was as clear as the luxury SUV's windshield.

She didn't want to alarm Shannon by reacting to the noise, so she ignored it. She couldn't focus much anyway because of her crack withdrawals. The noise was nothing but a nuisance.

The SUV rolled past another neighborhood at a leisurely pace. The city was now consumed by the darkness. The streets were illuminated by the lampposts at regular intervals. Kids and their guardians walked from house-to-house, collecting candy in their bags. They drove past a few police cruisers, but the cops didn't notice the hostage situation.

Eyes on the road, Shannon said, "So, we're almost to the bank. It's just down Main Street."

"I know where the bank is."

"Yeah, of course you do," Shannon said with a nervous, twitchy smile. "You must have lived around here for a while, right? I don't think I've seen you around."

"*Don't* look at me. Keep your eyes on the road."

"Y–Yeah, yeah, of course."

Crystal feared Shannon would recognize her from their short encounter at the grocery store if she took more than a couple of seconds to examine her. She covered half of her face with the wig and kept her head down. Despite the violent home invasion, Shannon didn't hate Crystal or the other intruders. She was trying to be friendly.

She asked, "So, how are things going at the house?"

Crystal heard the Cohen sisters sobbing as well as Patrick's raspy breathing. She said, "Fine."

"Can I listen?"

"No."

"But the young man, he said we could listen from–"

"I'll let you listen after you withdraw the cash without doing anything stupid. That's the deal. Okay? Now let's just... let's shut up and drive in peace."

Stopped at a red light, the interior of the vehicle was smothered by a tense silence. Crystal examined the decorated houses and picket fences around her. Shannon saw an opportunity to fight back. *Take the knife, then take the phone, then mute the call and jump out,* she thought. Then she spotted the droplet of blood rolling out of Crystal's nostril. Crystal didn't notice it until the blood touched her lip.

"Shit," she muttered.

Shannon said, "There's a handkerchief in my bag. Go ahead and use it."

"Yeah, okay."

Crystal took the lace handkerchief out of Shannon's purse. She wiped the blood off her face. It was smeared on her nose and lips, painting her skin pink. Nosebleeds were common in children and teenagers, usually caused by dry air, nose-picking, ongoing allergies, and frequent colds. Shannon was a good, observant mother, so she understood that. She also knew nosebleeds were caused by accidents, physical fights, and drug abuse. She had seen it before in the drug-addicted transients at the homeless shelter. She connected the pieces.

They drove off as the red light turned green.

Shannon said, "I understand why you're doing this. I wish it didn't have to be like this, but I get it. You feel like the world has treated you unfairly, like you've been pushed into a corner, like you have no other option but to fight and run. I'm not a psychic, I'm not going to pretend like I know your home situation or everything about you, but I know—*I know*—you're struggling with addiction right now. There are rehabilitation centers around town. A lot of discreet, helpful resources that won't charge you a dime to get started."

Crystal curled her lip at her and said, "You don't know shit about me. I'm not some–some kid you heard about in your gossip circles or that you saw in an infomercial. Stop fucking with me. I'll fuck back. You stupid, stupid bitch."

"You don't mean that, honey."

"What? What's that supposed to mean?"

"I'm not trying to push your buttons. You're holding my family hostage so that would be stupid of me. But I see a good girl in your eyes. You remind me of my daughter, Jill. If you took that wig off, you'd probably look like her, too. But... she's not an addict, and I see the addiction in your eyes, too. I'm not a doctor, but I've spoken to dozens of addicts throughout my life. Withdrawals are tough, aren't they? They make you feel sick and angry and depressed. So, I don't blame you for insulting me or threatening me at a time like this. I just want you to know: you're not alone."

Crystal was awed by Shannon's sympathy. Her younger brother stabbed the woman's husband in a plan concocted by her drug-dealing boyfriend. Then, without her knowledge, her boyfriend tortured Patrick again. Crystal wanted to hate Shannon for her compassion, she wanted to see her as a pretentious, arrogant fraud, but she felt the sincerity behind her words. Unlike the crew of criminals, Shannon was a genuinely good person.

As the car rolled to a stop at another red light, Shannon said, "I hope you understand: what you're doing is wrong. If you get caught, this will change your life forever. No good will come out of this."

"You don't think I know that?" Crystal responded, tears welling in her eyes. "But there's no good behind me anyway! I'm stuck! I can't turn back! Do you think I wanted to do this? You think I asked for this? I told you already: you don't know shit about me. You wouldn't understand because you... you're like an alien to me. You're so fucking rich and–and privileged that you're, like, from a different planet or something! But you watch us and you talk about us so you *think* you get it. You don't, okay? You don't know what it's like to be beaten by your dad *every day* of your life for over four years. Or to learn how to do drugs from your mom so you can block out the pain, too. Or to kill your dreams and work at a fast food restaurant to make a *fraction* of what your husband makes. And it's all because you got lucky and I didn't. You don't know how that feels and you never will. Your kindness... It's not going to stop a thing."

They sat in silence again, gazing into each other's eyes. Crystal was surprised to see Shannon was also crying. The fierce, honest speech broke her heart.

The driver behind them honked as the light turned green. He honked again and again, as if that would expedite their reaction.

As she drove off, Shannon said, "I'm sorry."

"Why? You didn't put me in this position, did you?"

"But you hate me because–"

"Never mind," Crystal interrupted. "I don't want to talk about this anymore. If I do, I'll get angry and I'll do something I'll regret. Let's just withdraw the money, go back to your place, and then split ways. I don't need your pity or your friendship. It's better this way."

"Okay, okay..."

Shannon wanted to lead Crystal and her friends to the light, but she knew she couldn't drag her out of the darkness against her will. At the end of the day, the decision fell on Crystal's shoulders. And Crystal only wanted the money. They took a right onto Main Street. They drove past hordes of teenagers and young adults loitering outside of *Oro Center*, waiting for the big party to begin. The street was congested with traffic, but the bank was only a few blocks away. They were close to the halfway mark of the plan.

Chapter Eleven

Silence

Jared handed Cody the pistol and said, "If he gets up, shoot the older one. If he keeps fighting, shoot the kid. Then kill him."

Cody looked at the gun, then at Patrick, and then at Jared. The dumbfounded facial expression behind his mask said: *you can't be serious.* The situation was spiraling out of control. With the initial stabbing, he unwittingly set off a chain reaction of violence. He didn't know how to stop it, but he figured they would all be safer if he took the gun from Jared.

He placed the machete on the kitchen bar, then he took the pistol from Jared. He examined it with a set of inquisitive eyes, like a virgin leering at a stripper for the first time. He had never held a pistol before. It was small and light, but he was aware of its destructive power. He aimed it at the back of Patrick's head while keeping his finger away from the trigger.

He asked, "What are you going to do?"

"What do you think? I'm going to loot the place, retard," Jared responded. He grabbed the backpack from the floor behind the sofa. As he walked down the hall, he shouted, "And check up on our friends at the bank! If that bitch is causing any trouble, shoot her kids!"

Cody nodded reluctantly. He held the phone up to his ear. He heard the purring engine and his sister's heavy breathing. Everything was fine.

Patrick looked back at him and whispered, "Come

on, son. You have the phone and the gun now. You have the power to stop this. Call the cops... and end it before it's too late. I'm dying here."

"I told you to stay quiet, man. He fucked you up because you wouldn't shut up. Just... Just stay quiet. Please."

"You don't want to do this. I can see it in your eyes. You're not like that–"

"Come on, man, can you please just shut up already?" Cody pleaded in desperation.

Jared entered the master bedroom down the hall. The room was simple: a bed, two nightstands, a dresser, an entertainment center, a closet with blinds built into its door, and a private bathroom. Simplicity did not equal poverty, though. Cotton sateen sheets covered the bed. A surround sound system hung on the wall above the entertainment center, connected wirelessly to a couple of speakers. There were some earrings on the dresser, sparkling under the light. Photographs of their kids at various stages of their lives stood on their nightstands and clung to the walls.

"Oh, shit, this is a goldmine," Jared said as he stepped into the room.

Although everything in the room was worth tens of thousands of dollars, he knew he would only receive a fraction of that at pawnshops and black-market merchants. The cash from the bank was their seed money.

Jared tossed the earrings into the backpack, then he searched the dresser's drawers. He riffled through boxers, thongs, socks, and undershirts. He approached the bed, but he stopped upon spotting the television. He shook his head, as if to say: *no way, we can't take it with us.* He knelt down and checked under the bed. To his utter surprise, the space was clean and empty. He went to the closet. He ignored the clothes and crouched in front of the small safe mounted on the wall near the floor.

He said the pin aloud as he pressed the buttons: "Nine... One... Seven... Three... Five... *Zero.*"

He heard a *beep*, then the door cracked open. In the safe, he found a jewelry box, some computer hard drives, and a wad of cash held together by a rubber band. He opened the top-drawer of the jewelry box. He found himself staring at a collection of rings, earrings, necklaces, and bracelets. He dumped it all in his bag with a big, devious grin on his face. He thumbed through the cash—at least one-thousand five-hundred dollars in twenties, fifties, and hundreds. He stopped as he pulled the hard drives out.

A Hitachi Magic Wand was hidden at the back of the safe. Since it was locked up, he safely assumed it wasn't used for massages. It was a cordless vibrator used for pleasure. He put the hard drives in his bag—with plans of entering the blackmail business in the future—then he grabbed the vibrator and exited the bedroom.

He smirked and shouted, "I found your toy! Maybe we can have some fun later!"

He peeked into the room to his right. It was a clean bathroom with a walk-in shower and a spacious bathtub. He looked into the room to his left. It was a laundry room with a washing machine, a drying machine, and two storage cabinets.

"You have a beautiful house!" he shouted as he made his way down the hall. "A beautiful house and a beautiful family. You're one lucky son of a bitch!"

He checked the second room to his right. It was Jill's bedroom. From the doorway, he spotted shelves packed with textbooks and novels, a desk with a laptop and an iPad on top, and a vanity table with a ton of makeup. It was a neat, organized room. He opened a door across the hall.

The smile—that slick, treacherous smile—was wiped off his face.

The room was untidy and cluttered. Men's jeans and shirts flooded the floor, along with an empty gallon of water and some snack wrappers. A bulky computer under a desk emitted a red glow. It was an expensive gaming PC, and it was still powered on. He remembered the teenage male on the fridge's touchscreen panel.

It was Dustin's bedroom.

Jared marched into the living room. He threw the backpack and the vibrator on the floor. He punched Patrick's right shoulder. A moist *crunch* came out of the wound on his collarbone. Patrick screamed and covered the cut with his injured hand. So, Jared threw a jab at his hand, further damaging Patrick's broken bones while aggravating the wound on his shoulder.

"Why?!" Patrick cried out as the burning pain surged from his shoulders to his hands.

Jared raised his knee up to his stomach, then he stomped on Patrick's crotch. His heavy, steel-toe boot hit *everything* from his stabbed belly button to his scrotum. The cuts across his lower abdomen widened. Fresh streams of blood leaked out of them.

Patrick stopped crying. He held his breath until his face turned blood-red and veins protruded from his forehead and neck. Then he fainted. He fell over the seat beside him on the sofa.

The Cohen sisters wept in the corner.

Wake up, daddy, please wake up!

Cody stuttered, "Wha–What did you do that for?"

Jared stuck his fingers into his sweaty hair and said, "The bastards lied to us."

"A–About what?"

"Someone else lives here. Their son, I think. These sons of bitches lied to us!"

"S–So what happens now? Do we leave? Is he... Is he dead?"

"The motherfucker isn't dead, you idiot," Jared said. He lifted Patrick's upper body from the middle seat and pushed him back against the backrest. Jared slapped Patrick's cheek and said, "Wake up. Stop acting, you snake. Wake up!"

Patrick's eyes fluttered open. His head fell forward, his chin on his chest. His arms shuddered, overwhelmed by the pain. He stared down at his numb crotch. He felt as if an army of insects were marching across his genitals. The bottom of his shirt and the top of his jeans were drenched in blood. A bank of brain fog distorted his memories. He sat there and wondered if his penis was severed during that awful evening.

Jared slapped him gently and said, "Stay awake, motherfucker. If you fall asleep again, if you try anything stupid, I'll kill your girls. I will skull-fuck them in front of you. You understand me? *Stay awake*, you cunt."

"I–I'm a–awake."

"Then look at me."

Patrick's eyes wandered to his left. His vision was blurred, but he could see his daughters in the corner of the room. Their fear was raw—*emotional.* He looked Jared in the eye.

Jared said, "The problem with people like you—the rich, high-and-mighty-type—is: you underestimate the people below you. You think I'm stupid, right? 'Oh, he's a drug dealer. He's a criminal. He's a no-good thug. He doesn't know shit about anything.' But I'm *not* stupid. I saw the pictures on the fridge and I found the bedroom. Where's the boy?"

"Boy?" Patrick repeated with a furrowed brow.

Jared slapped him. The *whack* echoed through the house and even startled the girls. Patrick squeezed his eyes shut as he tasted the blood leaking out of his gums.

"The boy! Your son!" Jared shouted.

Cody said, "Hey, man, someone's going to hear you. We should–"

"Shut your mouth," Jared said. "You keep that gun on those girls and you shoot when I tell you."

"Wait, wait," Patrick said as he tried to find his bearings. "Don't hurt them. I'm sorry. My son... He's not a boy. He's twenty years old. So, he... he moved away already."

"He moved away? He doesn't live here anymore?"

"Tha–That's right. He's gone."

Jared puckered his lips and nodded. Aside from the incessant whimpering and hoarse breathing, the house was quiet.

Patrick said, "Please take our stuff and leave. Meet

your friend somewhere, leave my wife on the side of the road, and then take the SUV and... and get out of town. That's what you want, don't you? Please, son, I can't last much longer like this. I need an ambulance or... or my first-aid kit. Give me something to work with."

"You *really* think I'm stupid, don't you?" Jared said as he walked away from the sofa.

"I don't. I respect–"

"Don't lie to me," Jared interrupted. "Don't... Don't 'patronize' me. Yeah, I think that's the right word. You think you're smart, but you fucked with the wrong bull tonight."

He took the machete off the kitchen bar, then he returned to the sofa. He stood in front of Patrick. He held the blade up to Patrick's sweaty neck. The sharp blade nicked him.

He said, "The computer is on in his room. There are laptops and iPads and all that shit in all of the other rooms, so don't tell me you were in there working or playing video games. Where is he?"

"Shit, fuck me," Patrick muttered, a nervous smile stretching across his face.

"Where is he?!"

"They're going to hear us!" Cody shouted.

Ignoring him, Jared glared at Patrick and shouted, "If you don't answer me, I'm going to chop off your youngest daughter's head! I'll behead her right here and I'll force you to watch, old man! Where's your son?!"

"He's at the homeless shelter! He–He's volunteering... He won't be home until nine o'clock at the earliest. That's the truth, okay? Please don't hurt them. They didn't do anything wrong. They didn't lie to you, I did."

Jared raised the machete over his head. His arm was steady, his glare was cold. He swung it down at Patrick's neck.

"No!" Cody shouted as he aimed the pistol at Jared.

Jared stopped mid-swing. The blade missed Patrick's neck by less than half a foot. Patrick closed his eyes, flinched, and turned away. He didn't want to see it coming. He wanted to wrap his arms around his head, but he could barely move them without aggravating his broken clavicles. Tears oozed out of his sealed eyelids. Facing death, he could only think about his family.

Jared scowled at Cody while breathing deeply through his nose. He was furious. He believed Cody was still fighting his conscience, but he doubted his resolve. *He won't pull the trigger,* he told himself in confidence. He raised the machete over his head again, then he swung down. He heard Cody's shout, but he didn't stop himself.

Instead of aiming for his neck, Jared swung at Patrick's left hand. With the chop, he severed Patrick's index, middle, and ring fingers. His pinky was sliced. It dangled down to his palm, barely attached, as he lifted his hand. The tip of his thumb was cut off, too. The tip of his thumb fell off the sofa while the rest of his severed fingers stayed on the cushion beside the blade.

Patrick cried as he wrapped the costume's cowboy vest around his mutilated hand. The pain emanating from his shoulders couldn't compete with the amputation. The girls kept screaming. Jill stood up, but she fell to the ground as soon as Jared swung the machete at her. He missed her by over a meter, but he wasn't trying to hit her anyway.

His words slurred by the pain, Patrick yelled, "No! Don't! Oh my God! No!"

Jared tossed the machete at the floor near the backpack and shouted, "Everyone, shut up! I want some peace and quiet! If you don't shut up in five seconds, you all die! I'm done fucking around! Five, four, three..." The chaos dwindled to some whimpers, groans, and mutters. Jared said, "That's more like it. Hey, retard, get on the phone and tell your sister to make sure they get back here by eight. They've got less than an hour and a half. Don't tell her about the son unless she already heard it. I don't want the mom to know that we know about him."

"O-Okay..." Cody responded.

While Cody updated his sister on the situation, Jared went to Jill's bedroom. He took the black pillowcases off of two pillows, then he returned to the living room. Kimberly shrieked as Jared placed a pillowcase over her head. She squirmed, jerking left-and-right, but she couldn't dodge him. She could have removed the pillowcase herself, but she was afraid of defying him. Jill grabbed his forearm and tried to pull him away, but to no avail. The young man was too strong. He grabbed a fistful of Jill's hair and tugged on her head.

Her muffled shout barely seeped past the duct tape: *Stop!*

"What are you doing to them?!" Patrick barked, his raspy voice breaking like a teenager's.

Jared smashed the side of Jill's head against the

wall—once, *twice*. She was dazed by the blows. He forced her head into the second pillowcase, then he pushed her back beside her little sister. The siblings could barely see through the cotton sateen pillowcases. The light in the room helped. They accepted the pillowcases as a gift and a curse. On one hand, they didn't have to see their father's grotesque wounds. On the other, the darkness left them feeling more vulnerable and lonely.

While Jared went to the kitchen, Patrick said, "Leave... Leave them out of it. I told you: they're innocent."

"They're innocent?" Jared repeated as he looked through the drawers. "Well, we're about to change that."

"What? Hey, please leave... leave them alone," Patrick said. He gazed into Cody's eyes and said, "Stop him. Please..."

Cody considered it for a second: *shoot him, then walk away.* But it was only a second. He walked away from the couch. He stood near the hall leading to the other rooms. He aimed the pistol at the floor while holding the cell phone up to his ear. He thought if he saw the scenario from a different angle that things would magically change.

Carnage always looked the same.

Jared returned to the living room with a spoon. He took a baggie of black tar heroin, a lighter, and a hypodermic needle out of his backpack. Patrick's eyes widened as he spotted the drug paraphernalia. He leaned forward, but he fell back against the seat before he could stand up. The pain across his torso was too intense.

"Don't," he croaked out.

Jared placed the sticky black heroin on the spoon. He ignited the lighter, then he held it under the spoon. The heroin melted slowly. The girls saw the lighter's flame through the thin pillowcases, but they didn't recognize the vinegary stench of the heroin. Jared pulled on the needle's plunger, sucking the black heroin into the barrel.

Patrick said, "I'm begging you. Don't do it. They're kids!"

"Relax. Chances are, they've done it already," Jared responded, eyes on the syringe.

"They're innocent!"

"If you think they're really innocent, then you're stupider than you look."

Jared grabbed Jill's upper arm with a tight grip, digging his thumb into her bicep. She screamed and wiggled against the wall, cornered.

"Stop it!" Patrick yelled. He fell over the middle seat again. His severed fingers rolled off the couch and hit the floor with three rapid *thuds.* He cried, "Oh God! Someone do something!"

Jared penetrated Jill's basilic vein at the crook of her elbow. He pushed down on the plunger, shooting half of the heroin into her bloodstream, then he pulled the needle out. A droplet of blood rolled out of the injection site. Jill shrieked as she felt a burning sensation across her arm. It felt as if Jared had injected her with some type of acid—and the acid was rapidly spreading across her limb.

Then, after ten seconds, she was hit with a wave of euphoria. The back of her head hit the wall behind her. She tilted her head back and looked at the ceiling through the pillowcase. The heat subsided, replaced with a welcomed warmth. She felt like a child tucked into bed with a warm blanket by her caring mother. Under the tape, she smiled.

Jared grabbed Kimberly's left foot. She tried to kick him, but she could barely move her legs.

Blobs of drool dripping from his mouth, Patrick shouted, "No! No! No! Not the feet! Please, not the feet!"

Jared raised his brow and glanced over his shoulder. He heard the panic in Patrick's voice. He was more afraid than ever before. Patrick understood the dangers of drug abuse. Injecting heroin between the toes led to increased chances of amputation and death. He didn't believe his precious thirteen-year-old daughter could handle it. At that moment, the needle was equivalent to a loaded gun.

"Alright, alright," Jared said, smirking. "I guess you prefer the arm, too."

Wheezing between each word, Patrick cried, "Just... leave... her... alone."

Jared injected the rest of the heroin into the basilic vein of Kimberly's left arm. The young girl cried at first, then she felt the rush of euphoria, and then she nodded off with her head on her sister's shoulder. *Dead silence*—the house was finally quiet.

"Why would you do something like this?" Patrick asked, defeat in his voice. "They didn't do anything to hurt you. You know it's true. We're... We're just a regular family. Because we have more money? Because I was rude to you? Because you... you wanted to prove a point?"

"All of the above," Jared responded. "And I'm not

done yet."

"Don't hurt them. Hurt me."

Jared huffed at him. Eighty-percent of the man's yellow button-up shirt was soaked in blood. His left hand didn't fare much better. His pinky was detached during his struggle, and he didn't even notice it. He was a bloody mess. Another act of torture would have brought him to the brink of death. It wasn't his time—*yet*.

Jared said, "They won't feel any pain. Only pleasure."

"Excuse me?"

Teary-eyed, Cody whispered, "Please don't do it. Please don't do it. Please don't do it."

He couldn't muster the courage to shout at him. He leaned back against the wall behind him, his arms down to his sides. He saw the object in Jared's hand—and it terrified him. It wasn't another gun, a knife, a hammer, or a crowbar. It was Shannon's vibrator.

Jared flicked the cordless vibrator's switch to its first level of intensity. Patrick immediately recognized the *buzzing* sound.

"Stay away from them, goddammit!" Patrick barked.

He fell off the sofa. The floorboards rattled as he landed on his knees. He felt a knot in his stomach due to the insufferable pain surging from the stab wounds across his lower abdomen. He shimmied forward, inch by inch.

"Hurt me!" he barked. "I'm right here!"

Cody stepped forward and stuttered, "Ja–Ja–Jar..." He stopped before he could say his name. He said, "You can't do that, man. The–The phone... They can hear you."

"Mute the mic," Jared said.

"But what if–"

"*Now.*"

Patrick yelled, "Shoot him! Just shoot him al–"

Jared kicked Patrick's jaw, like a man punting a football. Patrick was knocked unconscious. A gash stretched across his jawline. He awoke fifteen seconds later. He glanced over at Cody. He saw the teenager muting the phone's mic while shaking like a wet dog during a powerful storm. He looked at Jared. Through his blurred vision, he saw Jared rubbing the vibrator against Kimberly's shin.

"Feels good, doesn't it?" Jared asked.

He rubbed the head of the wand against her knees, then slowly up her thigh, and then it disappeared under her dress. The girl whimpered while fading in-and-out of consciousness.

Patrick could only watch in terror as his daughters were molested in front of him. Cody couldn't stop himself from crying. He delved into a new layer of Jared's depravity.

Chapter Twelve

Withdrawals

With the phone to her ear, Crystal sat in the passenger seat and stared at Shannon. She clenched her jaw and breathed deeply through her nose. She heard the begging, the arguing, and the torture. She recognized the *buzz* of the vibrator, too. The call was muted now, but she acted as if she were still communicating with her crew—as if all hell hadn't broken loose at the Cohen house.

The SUV rolled to a stop in front of the bank. A few people lined up at the ATMs outside of the building—some wearing costumes, others wearing casual clothing.

Crystal blinked erratically—fast but inconsistent—as she snapped out of her trance. She had to grunt to clear her throat.

Talking at the phone, she said, "Okay, we're here. She's getting ready to head out right now." The call remained silent. She turned her attention to Shannon and said, "You go in there and you ask for *nine-thousand five-hundred* dollars. If you ask for more, they'll call the manager and then they'll ask you a hundred fucking questions and then they'll have to report it all to the government. We don't want that."

"I understand."

"How much are you withdrawing?"

"Nine-thousand five-hundred dollars."

"Good girl. And why are you making that withdrawal?"

"To... To buy Jill a car. I'm paying in cash."

"You're a good fucking girl, you know that?"

Shannon nodded reluctantly. She took her wallet out of her bag. She drew one deep breath after another, like an actor before a big performance.

Crystal said, "Hurry up. We need to get home before eight."

"Eight? Why? What's wrong?"

"Nothing's wrong, but... we've got a bus to catch if we're going to get out of this town. Withdraw the money. If I see the manager—or anyone that *looks* like a manager—come anywhere near you or the clerk, I'll tell my friends at your house and your family will suffer. We just want the money. Okay? Don't do anything stupid."

Shannon doubted Crystal's story about the bus, but she refused to confront her with her family's safety at stake. She took one last breath, then she climbed out of the SUV. Fear had a funny way of changing people. On any other day, she would have felt silly entering her bank in a Bo Peep costume. That night, she was willing to do *anything* to save her family.

She waited in line behind an elderly woman. Hands on her walker, the frail woman looked back at her, ran her eyes over her costume, then she smiled and winked at her.

Shannon returned the smile, although she was fighting the urge to cut in front of her in line. The elderly woman was called to one of the tellers. She waved at Shannon, then she dragged her walker to the counter. Shannon stepped forward. She waited for five minutes, arms crossed and foot tapping.

Another teller beckoned to her. The name tag on her shirt read: *Caroline Caruso*.

Shannon approached the counter and said, "Hello, I'd like to make a withdrawal."

"Sure, I can help you with that," Caroline responded. "Which account are we withdrawing from today?"

Crystal watched the conversation from the passenger seat of the SUV. She looked at the cell phone's screen. She was relieved to see that the call was still connected, but she couldn't hear a thing.

Speaking directly at the mic, she said, "Hello? Hey, can you hear me? I can't hear you guys anymore. What's happening over there?" There was no response. She said, "I know you're there, brat. What happened? Is everything okay? Come on, guys, don't do this to me now. We're so fucking close. I'm at the bank. She's getting the money. Did you hear me? Huh? Damn it, answer me!"

No one answered.

She sighed in frustration and glanced around. She examined the customers lined up at the ATMs. From afar, she saw their wads of cash as they stuffed the money into their wallets and departed. She thought about robbing them with the knife and using the cash to buy more crack. She closed her eyes and shook her head. *No, no, no,* she told herself, *stick to the plan.*

She looked out the passenger door window. She spotted a police cruiser parked in front of a Rite-Aid across the parking lot. The officer appeared to be dormant or working on his mobile data terminal.

She reclined the seat and said, "Cody, I'm getting nervous here. If you can hear me, give me some sort of sign. What did Jared do to them? What's going on over there?" The call remained quiet. She muttered, "Oh, shit... Damn it... What am I supposed to do? You guys have to answer me or... or I'm leaving. I'm sorry, Cody, but... if I have to, I'll leave you behind. Say something. Please..."

Once again, there was no response.

Caroline counted the cash in front of Shannon, then she secured the bills with a currency strap. It was almost half an inch thick. She placed the money and a receipt in a thick envelope. She slid it across the counter.

She said, "Thank you for your business, Mrs. Cohen. I hope you'll–"

"I have to tell you something," Shannon interrupted in a low voice. "But you have to act natural, okay? You can't make a big scene or something *very* bad will happen. We're being watched from my SUV out there. I'm in a whole lot of trouble and I could sure use some help."

Caroline froze in fear. Her eyes darted to the left. She spotted the SUV in the parking lot, but she could barely see the passenger. She caught a glimpse of the orange wig, though. She reached for the phone beside her keyboard.

Shannon said, "Don't call anyone. If she sees you, she'll hurt my family. There are men at my house, miss. If anyone else comes close to you or if you make a scene, she'll tell her friends to hurt them. I don't want that. I just... I... I don't know what I want. They said they'd leave as soon as we got home with the money. Maybe you can call the police after I leave and ask a cop to look after us until *they* get out of my house? Something like that?"

"Okay, ma'am. We have protocols for situations like this. I'm going to message my manager on the computer. He'll call the cops and we'll work from there. One second please."

Shannon and Caroline smiled at each other. From the outside looking in, it appeared as if they were finishing up by reviewing the transaction. In the bank, they looked as nervous as teenagers on their first date. Crystal couldn't see much from her position, but she didn't notice any suspicious people near the teller. The guard in the bank—standing near the entrance—scratched the back of his neck and yawned. It was business as usual.

Time moved at a snail's pace. Seconds felt like minutes, and minutes like hours. Fifteen minutes passed since the envelope was placed on the counter.

Crystal raised the phone to her ear and said, "I think she's planning something. What do I do? Hello? Cody? Jared? Goddammit, you guys are assholes! Where are you?!"

In the bank, Caroline said, "I'm being told that the cops will create a perimeter around your neighborhood. As long as you're not in any immediate danger, they want you to continue to follow their directions. The police will be following you from a distance to ensure your safety and they'll be watching your house to ensure the safety of your family. That's all we can do for you from here. I'm sorry, and I'm praying for the best. I really am."

Shannon sniffled and said, "I can't thank you enough. Please... Please smile so she won't get suspicious."

"Of course, ma'am," Caroline said as a welcoming smile stretched across her face. She slid the envelope closer to Shannon and said, "Have a nice day, ma'am."

"You too."

Shannon shoved the envelope into her bag. She swiped at the tears clinging to her eyes, she took a deep breath, then she marched out of the bank. She returned to the driver's seat of the SUV.

"Do you want it now?" she asked as she placed her bag on the center console.

Scowling at her, Crystal asked, "What the hell took you so long?"

"It took them a while to get the money and count it."

"I saw them give you the envelope a while ago. Ten, fifteen minutes ago."

"Then I had to answer some questions about the withdrawal. That's all, really."

Crystal scanned the bank and the parking lot. She didn't notice anything out of the ordinary. The guard didn't peek over at them and the cop continued to relax during his break.

She said, "Drive. Go back to your place."

They drove out of the parking lot without arousing any suspicion. They retraced their steps and headed back to the Cohen house. As Shannon switched lanes, Crystal puked. The greenish-brown vomit struck the dashboard, then it splattered on the windshield, the passenger window, and Crystal's jeans. She retched, then she hiccupped, then she vomited again. She puked straight down on her lap.

Shannon said, "Oh God. I'll pull over."

"Don't," Crystal said, hiccupping. "Go... home."

"You're sick, hun. I can–"

"I don't need your damn help! And I'm not your 'hun,' okay?! Stop treating me like your daughter 'cause you're not my mom. Take us to your house. I'll clean this up before we get there, I promise."

Shannon saw the symptoms of crack withdrawals taking a toll on Crystal—eating away at her from the inside. Crystal was frail, lightheaded, and nauseous. Again, Shannon thought about overpowering her, disarming her while yanking the phone out of her hand and quickly muting the mic, but she couldn't smother her sympathetic heart. She felt nothing but pity for her.

In the back of her mind, a part of her wanted her to succeed in the robbery—as long as her family wasn't harmed any further. She was cheering for her.

She asked, "Aren't you going to tell your friends about the money?"

"I–I, um… I told them while you were walking out of the bank."

"Well, what did he say? Is everything okay back home?"

I have no idea—Crystal had to stop herself from blurting out the truth. She heard the arguments and the violence, but, like Shannon, she was out of the loop.

She said, "Everything's fine. Just drive."

Chapter Thirteen

Playtime

"Oh my God, you monster," Patrick cried. "How could you... do this to them? They never hurt... a soul. They helped people... They were innocent..."

He sat on the floor and leaned back against the sofa. He watched as Jill convulsed and moaned, and he listened to the *buzz* of the vibrator as it drilled into his ears. Debilitated by the pain and incapable of abandoning his daughters, he was forced to watch their orgasms—one after the other. The heroin fooled them into feeling pleasure, but fear and anxiety also ran through their veins. It was unnatural to them.

It was molestation, *it was rape,* and, deep down, they knew that very well.

Jared turned off the vibrator. Except for the ragged breathing and constant sniffling, the house was quiet.

Crouched in front of the girls, he looked at Patrick, he smirked, and he said, "That was hot."

"Fuck you!" Patrick roared.

Jared flinched jokingly, then he said, "Wow, looks like you've still got some fight in you. You really love these girls, don't you?"

"Fuck you..."

"I'll be honest with you. I'm growing a little attached to them. I know I said we'd leave as soon as we got the money, that no one else would get hurt, but..."

Patrick shook his head and said, "Don't you even think about it."

"I just can't leave without having some fun," Jared continued. "These girls got me going crazy, man. My dick is about to tear through my pants. Hard as hell, pops, *hard as hell.*"

Patrick whimpered as he leaned forward. He tried to get on his hands and knees, but he fell to his side beside the coffee table. Saliva frothed on his lips and mucus dripped from his nose. He was hysterical.

He shouted, "Please! Leave them alone! I'll give you anything!"

"I want the girls."

"No, no, no, no! Please, son! I'm begging you!"

Jared said, "There's nothing you can do to stop me. You shouldn't have lied." While Patrick begged, Jared approached Cody and said, "Give me the gun."

Webs of red veins covering his eyes, Cody stared at Jared, then at the pistol in his right hand. He stood there with his arms down to his sides—speechless, motionless, *useless.* He wasn't harmed, it didn't happen to him, but the sexual assault paralyzed him. When it came to violence and sex, he didn't have any experience.

Cody raised the pistol, finger on the trigger. He felt as if he were moving in slow-motion. *Shoot him in the leg,* he thought, *no, the stomach.* Before he could aim it at his chest, Jared took the pistol out of his hand. He tucked it into the back of his waistband. He yanked the cell phone out of Cody's other hand. The call was still connected. He held it up to his ear. He heard someone breathing.

Jared threw the phone on the console table and said, "Don't ever aim a gun at me again. We're on the same side, remember?"

"Y–Yeah…"

"Do you want to have some fun?"

"Y–Yeah," Cody stuttered again, repeating himself as if he were programmed to do so. He said, "Wait. No, I can't."

Jared smirked and said, "Don't be stupid. You said 'yeah,' so *something* inside of you wants to get in on the fun."

"No, it was an acci–"

"It's alright, little man. Just follow your gut. Come on, let's get them to their rooms. We can have some 'playtime' with 'em before your sister gets home."

From the ground, Patrick shouted, "Don't listen to him!"

Jared patted Cody's shoulder and said, "Come on, at least give me a hand. You don't want them to get away, do you? Then we'd *really* be in deep shit."

Cody thought about his options. *Fight him?* Without the gun, he was powerless. He couldn't stand toe-to-toe against an armed maniac. *Talk him down?* He saw the devilish look in Jared's eyes. The young man was stuck in his ways. *Stand still?* Jared wasn't a wild animal. He preyed on everyone in the house, regardless of their friendliness or hostility.

"Can I talk to my sister?" Cody asked, choking back his tears.

"*No.*"

"B–But–"

"She's busy. Come on, help me get them to their rooms."

Jared handed Cody the roll of duct tape, then he pulled him away from the wall. They approached the girls in the corner. Jared lifted Kimberly's limp body from the floor, as if he were carrying his bride on their wedding day. Kimberly groaned and twitched in his arms. Eyes narrowed to slits, she saw nothing but darkness under the pillowcase.

"Dad... Daddy," she said, barely audible.

She was taken to her bedroom. A mural was painted on the black accent wall behind her bed. It was the Red Door from the *Insidious* movie. She painted it with her mother a year ago. Her parents supported and nurtured her interest in horror fiction. She was, in fact, an innocent child.

"Creepy fuckin' room," Jared muttered. He set her down at the foot of the bed. He glanced back and found Cody standing in the doorway—*terrified.* Jared said, "Give me the tape."

Cody said, "What are you going to-"

"Just hand it over already."

Cody sighed in disappointment. He followed Jared's instructions and handed him the roll of duct tape. Over the tape on her wrists, Jared taped Kimberly's arms to one of the bedposts at the foot of the bed. He cut the tape around her ankles with the chef's knife—the same knife he used to stab Patrick's collarbone. He opened her legs and looked up her dress. He couldn't help but lick his lips as he leered at her panties.

He said, "This one's mine."

"*What?*" Cody asked.

Jared walked out of the room without saying another word. In the living room, Patrick wiggled his way to his oldest daughter. He made it around the coffee table and closer to the recliner, leaving a trail of blood behind him. He was three meters away from her, but he felt like he'd have to crawl across a continent to reach her.

"Leave her," Patrick said while holding his breath. "Please."

Ignoring him, Jared shouted, "Give me a hand over here!"

Cody returned to the living room. Jared hooked his arms under Jill's armpits, then he beckoned to Cody, as if to say: *grab her legs.* Again, despite his heart telling him to stop, Cody's survival instincts forced him to follow Jared's orders. He grabbed her legs and then they lifted her from the floor and carried her out.

As he watched them, Patrick cried, "Don't take my daughter! Oh God!"

In Jill's room, the home invaders repeated the process: they set her down on the floor near the foot of the bed, they taped her arms to one of the bedposts, and then they cut the tape around her ankles to free her legs.

"She's a beauty, isn't she?" Jared asked as he stood beside Cody. He patted the teenager's shoulder and asked, "What do you think? You wanna fuck her?"

Wide-eyed, Cody asked, "What? No! I can't do some–"

"Hey, relax, kid," Jared said, chuckling. "This would be your first time, right?"

"I'm not doing it."

"But, *if* you did, it would be your first, right?"

Cody clenched his jaw and shook his head. The answer was obvious: *yes*. But he didn't want to discuss his virginity with a psychopath in front of one of his classmates. He turned around and headed to the door. Jared grabbed his shoulder and pulled him back. He kept his arm around him to stop him from running out.

"Listen, man, you can't keep running from shit like this," Jared said. "You're not going to survive out there in the real world if you can't do something as simple as fuck a bitch. You'll end up holding us back... and I can't have that. So, I want you to fuck her. I don't care if you nut after three, two, or even one thrust. You're going to fuck her."

"I–I can–can't... I, um... If I... If I cum inside her, they'll, um..."

"Don't worry about that. Here, use this."

Jared pulled his wallet out, then he took a condom out of the coin pocket. He handed it to him. Cody accepted it. He stared at it with tears in his eyes. His parents neglected him, but he always expected his father to give him the 'sex talk' as well as his first condom. It felt wrong in Jill's bedroom. They were talking about *raping* a drugged woman. It wasn't the special moment of his innocent fantasies.

"Fuck her," Jared said.

Cody said, "I don't think I–"

"What are you scared of? Are you a faggot or something? Look at those legs, *those tits,*" Jared said. He pulled the pillowcase off her head, then he yanked the tape off her mouth. He continued, "That face. That mouth. Damn, look at those dick-sucking lips. This bitch is perfect. Sexy as fuck."

Cody ran his eyes over her body—from her sweaty brown hair to her soft breasts, from her wide hips to her small, pedicured feet. He was attracted to her. He saw her as the most beautiful girl at his school. But he hesitated.

Jared said, "If you won't fuck her, then I will. Then I'll kill her, I'll kill you, and... and I'll kill your sister when she comes back with the money. If I can't trust you, I can't trust her. What's it going to be?"

Cody's breathing intensified. His throat and chest were tight, and he felt like his intestines were squirming inside of him, as if there were snakes in his belly. He took off his mask and tried to calm himself. He looked at Jill. He bit his bottom lip as he stared at her crotch. He couldn't lie to himself: he was aroused by her orgasm in the living room.

I'm doing this to survive, he told himself, *I'm doing this because he's making me.* At heart, he knew he was lying to himself. He was a deviant—like Jared, like his sister, like his father, like his mother. He couldn't escape his fate. His fingers trembled as he unbuckled his pants. His penis was erect, pushing up against his boxers.

"Yeah, you get that pussy, little man," Jared said, pride glimmering in his eyes. He nodded at the condom and asked, "You know how to put that on?"

Cody stuttered, "I–I can do it." He looked at the condom, then at his dick, and then at Jill. He asked, "Should I take off her clothes first?"

"Yeah, that's probably a good idea."

Cody crouched in front of her. His face scrunched up as if he were about to cry, he pulled her pajama shorts down. His cock grew upon spotting the ribbon on her baby blue panties. There was a wet spot on her underwear, too. It was a natural reaction to stimulation. She wasn't aroused by the molestation, but she couldn't control her bodily fluids. He hooked his fingers under the waistband of her panties. Her underwear barely reached her thighs before he gasped and shook. He was surprised by her hairless crotch. He had seen plenty of porn before, but it was different in person.

Grinning, Jared said, "Keep going." Cody gulped loudly as he removed her underwear. Jared said, "You can keep that as a souvenir if you want."

Cody threw the underwear under the bed. He glanced back at the door. He thought about Jill, the rest of the Cohen family, and his own sister. He could tell right from wrong—and he was *so* wrong in Jill's bedroom. He heard Patrick's weeping and begging in the living room. Tears dripped from Cody's eyes with each blink. The panic returned with full force, sending jolts of anxiety through his body. Yet, he remained fully erect. His heart said 'no' while his body shouted 'yes!' On his knees, he stared up at Jared again, hoping he would either shoot him and put him out of his misery or help him rape Jill so he wouldn't have to do it by himself.

Jared said, "Don't pussy out now. You've got fresh pussy right in front of you. You can do it, little man."

Cody closed his eyes and gave him a nod, a single tear rolling down his rosy cheek. He opened the condom wrapper. The condom was dry and brittle, but he didn't notice. It was his first time holding a condom. His dick flopped out as he pulled his boxers down. He rolled the condom down to the base of his penis. He scooted forward until his knees were under her thighs. His dick was less than half a foot away from her crotch. He leaned over her, his face close to hers.

He gazed into her eyes. Jill squinted back at him. She recognized him from their school, but she questioned herself. The drug led to sudden bursts of happiness as well as bouts of confusion and anxiety. Her body didn't know how to react to the heroin. She thought she was hallucinating or dreaming. She couldn't even remember the events before the home invasion. Her mind was addled, thoughts melting into each other. The tears in her eyes blurred her vision, too.

In a slow, weak voice, she asked, "Do I know you?"

"I'm sorry," Cody whispered. "He–He'll kill us all if I don't do this."

"Kill... Kill us?"

Cody sniffled and nodded.

Jill said, "Save... my sister."

"I–I'll do my best."

"Fuck her already," Jared demanded. "Jesus Christ, kid, you're not going to marry her. Get it over with."

By then, Cody's dick turned flaccid. He rubbed it against her wet labia. He thrust it at her, but his dick slid across her bald pubic area. He thrust it again at her crotch, poking her with it. After a few seconds, he grew erect again. He penetrated her with the next thrust. Patrick's shouts and Jared's body vanished. Most of the furniture disappeared, too.

It was only Cody, Jill, and the bed.

As deep as possible, Cody forced his penis into her. His arms shook while a coat of sweat covered his brow. He pulled his hips back, then he thrust into her again. He felt a rush of euphoria and a pleasant warmth across his body, as if someone had injected heroin into his basilic vein. He couldn't help but smile. He was having sex with his crush. His dream came true.

To his dismay, it only lasted twenty seconds and six thrusts. His eyes rolled, his limbs trembled, and his ass tightened as he ejaculated. With a loud, satisfied sigh, he returned to the real world. He heard Patrick's crying and Jared's laughter. He saw the tears pooling in Jill's dim, droopy eyes. He noticed each twitch of her runny nose, dried lips, and flushed cheeks.

Despite the heroin in her system, Jill didn't feel any pleasure from the sex. She felt violated and betrayed. Her body was *invaded* and *desecrated* by two young men.

Cody pulled his dick out of her. He fell onto his ass and scooted back. The reservoir tip of the condom was filled with his semen. Some of it leaked out from a crack on the crisp condom. He struggled to his feet and lifted his pants up while pulling the condom off. He glanced at every corner of the room, searching for somewhere to hide the used rubber.

He asked, "Wha–What do I do? Oh, shit, I–I think it broke. Look, it–it's leaking. They're going to find it and I'm going–"

"*Relax*," Jared said, still chuckling. "Throw it in the kitchen sink. We'll take it with us after your sister comes back with the cash."

"Wha–What about her? Should I... clean her?"

"Don't worry about her. They're not going to find a drop of cum and, no, she's not going to get pregnant. You know how many times I've nutted in your sister without her getting pregnant? *A lot.*"

(Unbeknownst to him, Crystal underwent three

abortions in the last two years because of their unprotected sex.)

Cody put the hockey mask on. He took another step back and examined his victim. Jill nodded off, tears wetting her cheeks.

"What if she tells the cops?" Cody asked.

Jared patted his shoulder and said, "She's not going to tell anyone. She won't remember it. If she does, they either won't believe her 'cause of the black tar or she won't say a thing 'cause she'll be embarrassed. I mean, look at this family, little man. Look at the jewelry in my bag. They are *filthy* rich. They care about their *image* more than anything else. We're in the clear." He pushed him towards the door and asked, "So, how does it feel to be a man?"

Confusing, awful, terrifying—Cody didn't want to be a 'man' if rape was one of the requirements. He was haunted by Jill's face and tormented by his actions. He shambled through the living room, condom in hand. Patrick had crawled back to the space between the sofa and the coffee table. He dragged himself through puddles of his own blood. The mere sight of the used condom set a fire of rage ablaze in his eyes. He slammed his fist on the floorboard and roared.

He shouted, "You little bastard! You monster! I gave you a chance! I... I would have helped you! Oh God!! What did you do?"

Cody threw the condom into the sink. He stared at it with a set of hopeless eyes. He heard Patrick's words, but he ignored him. He rinsed the semen out of the condom, then he returned to the living room.

As the teenager walked past him, Patrick asked,

"Are they dead? Did you... Did you kill them?"

Cody clenched his jaw and jogged into the hall. The man's voice was killing him inside. He found Jared standing in the doorway leading to Kimberly's bedroom.

"What are you doing?" Cody asked.

"It's my turn to play."

"What?"

"You heard me."

Cody said, "Wait, wait, wait. What do you... Are you... You want to fu... fu..." *Fuck*—he couldn't say that word while talking about a thirteen-year-old girl. He asked, "You want to 'play' with *her?*"

Jared smirked at him and said, "I've never been with a girl like her. I just want to see what it's like, you know?"

"*No!* No, man, you can't do that!"

"What? Are you kidding me? You just *fucked* her sister in the other room and now you're going to pull this high-and-mighty bullshit on me?!"

"I–I made a mistake!"

Jared pushed him. Cody crashed into the wall beside the door to Jill's room. He looked down at himself. He didn't have a weapon. He looked down the hall. He spotted the backpack on the floor in the living room. He thought about using the hammer or the machete against Jared, but he knew he couldn't beat him.

One bullet from the pistol would have taken him down.

Jared glared at him and said, "I thought you were a man. I thought you were growing up. Looks like you're still a pussy."

"I just don't think–"

"Well you don't have to think anymore. You just follow my orders. Go to the living room and make sure that old man doesn't escape or do anything stupid. I'll be in the room with the little one. I'll close the door and I'll try to keep it down, so I won't 'hurt your feelings' or anything like that, but I can't promise anything. I'll be done in ten, maybe fifteen minutes. Do you get me?"

Cody couldn't say a word. He could only shake and cry. Jared slapped Cody's mask, then he entered Kimberly's bedroom. His voice was muffled behind the door. He spoke to Kimberly with a gentle, understanding tone. Kimberly whimpered and groaned. The floorboards creaked and whined underneath them.

Cody removed his mask. His back against the wall, he covered his face with both hands and slid down to the floor. He was horrified by the experience and disappointed in himself. Patrick begged for information in the living room. The used condom gave him an idea of his daughters' plight, but he didn't know all of the details. Deep down, he didn't want to know. He didn't think he could handle it.

Chapter Fourteen

Hope in Hell

Patrick leaned back against the sofa with his feet under the coffee table. Blood was now splattered on his face and neck. Cody sat on the floor beside the backpack, his knees up to his face. He stared absently at the floor, reliving his awful actions in Jill's bedroom over and over again. The sound of a bed *thumping* against the wall was accompanied by Kimberly's muffled whimpers.

Without making eye contact, Patrick asked, "Did you kill her? Did you kill her after you... after you raped her?" Cody stayed silent. Patrick continued, "If she's alive, if *they're* alive, I can still forgive you."

Cody tilted his head and looked at the man. He wondered if he was sincere or if he was trying to manipulate him. He didn't seem like the manipulative-type, though. He didn't share the same sly, conniving spark in his eyes with Jared. Patrick looked back at him. His head shook in every direction due to the pain surging across every inch of his body.

He said, "Help me. Help... Help me save them."

"I can't. He has the gun."

"Call the cops."

Cody said, "I don't trust my..." He stopped before he could say 'sister.' He said, "If I hang up the phone, your wife might get hurt. Like, *badly* hurt."

"Shit."

They sat there without saying a word for thirty seconds, listening to the rhythmic *thumping* of the rape.

Patrick said, "Then help us get out of here."

"*I can't.* Don't you get it? It's impossible. He has a fucking gun. Your daughters are drugged. They're knocked out right now. You can barely move, and I don't think I can even carry one of them. We're stuck here until... until he says it's over."

Patrick said, "No. Listen, if you... if you help me get to the front door and help me down those porch steps, I *can* get help. I can reach a neighbor. I can find a trick r' treater. I can get us out of this. You just have to give me a hand... and you have to promise me something. I need your word that you'll... you'll protect my daughters as soon as he gets out of that room." His voice trembling, he said, "I don't want to abandon them, but this... Goddammit, this is the only way. I know you're not a bad kid. I know you don't want to be here. Please, help us before it's really too late. I'm begging you."

There were hints of sadness and anger in Patrick's voice, but Cody only noticed his sadness and desperation. If he had the chance, Patrick would have exacted his revenge and killed Cody for hurting his family.

Cody listened to the *thumping*—that *damn* thumping. He clenched his fists and grinded his teeth. He heard a loud, feminine *yelp*. It came from Kimberly's room. *He's hurting her,* he thought, *he's going to kill them and then we won't be able to escape any of this.* Their actions in the Cohen house were irreversible, but he saw a chance at redemption by helping the family.

He took off his mask and revealed his identity. He

swiped at the tears and mucus on his face, then he looked Patrick in the eye.

He said, "Move fast. You only have one chance."

"Thank you," Patrick said.

Cody rushed to his side. He wrapped his arm around his waist and tried to lift him up. Patrick hissed in pain as he struggled to his knees. He leaned against the sofa, planted his palm on the coffee table, then he pushed himself up to his feet—accidentally pushing the coffee table at the same time. The coffee table *screeched* on the floorboards.

Cody and Patrick stopped moving. They stared at the wall behind the entertainment center, then at the hallway. The *thumping* stopped. The *plop* of Patrick's dripping blood was the only sound in the house.

Five seconds passed.

Then ten seconds.

The *thumping* continued. Kimberly yelped again. Patrick fought the urge to barge into her room and fight Jared. He knew he couldn't win in his current condition.

"I'm sorry, baby," he whispered, fighting back his tears.

They hobbled around the sofa. Patrick bumped into the end table. The picture frame *clacked* as it fell over. They made their way to the entrance hall.

"Almost there," Cody said. "Don't scream when you get out there. If he–"

They froze. They heard jingling keys beyond the door. The lock on the knob unlocked with a *click*. The keys jingled again. Then the lock above the knob unlocked, too—*click!* The trespassers forgot to secure the deadbolt after Crystal departed with

Shannon. The door swung open.

Dustin walked into the house with his head down, music blaring from his Bluetooth earbuds. He kicked the door behind him. Before he could turn to lock it, he spotted his father—drenched in blood—standing beside a teenager. He didn't recognize the intruder. He removed his earbuds and stepped forward with caution.

"What is this?" he asked, awed. "Holy shit, dad, what did he... what happened to you?"

Patrick couldn't help but smile in relief. He fell out of Cody's arms and crashed into the wall to his right. He cried and laughed. He wanted to tell him everything, but he felt like his tongue was severed. There was so much to say, but he couldn't say a single word. *'They did this to me, your mother is being held hostage, your sisters were drugged and raped.'*—all of it was difficult to admit.

Dustin saw enough to panic, though. He saw the knocked over furniture, his father's mutilated hand and forearm, the blood on his father's clothing, the blood smeared on the walls, *the blood pooling on the living room floor.* He was only gone for a few hours, but it looked like a massacre had occurred at the house during his absence. His survival instincts told him to fight.

Cody held his hand up to Dustin and stuttered, "Wa-Wait. I-I can explain."

Dustin ran forward and tackled Cody. The air was knocked out of Cody as he hit the floor in the living room. Patrick stopped laughing. Relief turned to fear in the blink of an eye. He feared Jared would shoot his son if he were caught in the house.

"No," Patrick said, just below a shout. "Get out. Get help. *Run.*"

Dustin mounted Cody's waist. He swung down at Cody as quickly as possible, pounding his face with hammer fists, as if they were fighters in the Octagon. Cody tried to speak, but he could barely breathe. His cheeks and nose turned pink and then red. Blood leaked out of his nose and a cut stretched across his bottom lip.

Patrick shouted, "He's helping us!"

Dustin couldn't hear him in his fit of rage. He only heard the *thudding* of his fists as he struck Cody's face. Cody wrapped his arms around his head, so Dustin pounded away at his forearms. Dustin's fists slipped past Cody's defenses, too, allowing him to strike his chin, his cheeks, and his forehead a few more times. The beating left Cody disoriented, lightheaded, and horrified.

Between each hit, he said, "Please... I didn't... want to... do this."

Dustin punched his chin, loosening his lower incisors. Cody swung his head from side-to-side and kept his arms up, trying his best to block and dodge the punches, but he couldn't win. He was slower and weaker than Dustin, and Dustin benefited from hysterical strength. He was afraid for his father, *for his family*, so the adrenaline increased his stamina and his power. He was unstoppable.

Cody rationalized that he needed another unstoppable person to stop him—someone brave, someone strong, *someone armed.*

He said, "I'm sorry..."

Dustin didn't hear him. He grabbed a fistful of

Cody's hair, pushed his head back against the floorboard, then he hit his forehead with the bottom of his fist. Patrick heard him, though. He shook his head slowly. His eyes said: *please don't.*

Cody yelled "Help! Jared! Help me! He's in here!"

The thumping and whimpering in Kimberly's room stopped. Yet again, Dustin didn't notice it. He moved down and punched Cody's chest, putting all of his weight behind each jab. Cody lifted his knees up and lowered his arms to his chest while groaning with each punch. So, Dustin punched his face again. Cody's nasal septum was broken, crooked like a squiggly line.

A door in the hallway swung open and hit a wall in a bedroom—*bang!*

Dustin stopped pummeling Cody. He stared at the hallway, eyes wide with terror. He saw a killer clown—makeup smeared with sweat and blood. Cody saw his savior. His limp arms fell to his sides as he faded out of consciousness. Patrick screamed in pain as he stumbled towards his son and the young trespasser. He grabbed his son's shoulder with his good hand and tried to pull him away from Cody.

Dumbstruck by Jared's appearance in the house, Dustin stared at the intruder and whispered, "Who the hell are you? What did you do to my sister?"

"You're his son, aren't you?" Jared asked. He grinned, shook his head, and said, "You shouldn't have come here."

"What did you do to my sister?!" Dustin barked as he jumped up to his feet.

Patrick yelled, "Dustin, run! He has a gun!"

Dustin's stiff shoulders dropped, his mouth fell

open, and a short gasp escaped his lips. He wasn't a trained boxer, but fights were easy to start and end. Professional or amateur, veteran or newcomer, one lucky punch to the chin could change everything. He was willing to take the intruders' punches to save his family.

Guns were different. One lucky bullet could *kill* any person, and the human body was more fragile to bullets than punches. He could have died from a shot to the thigh. His survival instincts said: *you're no match for a gun, get the hell out of there!* But his body froze. Fear was a natural paralyzing agent. He stood there and watched as Jared ran towards him.

Jared pistol-whipped him. Dustin crashed into the wall beside him, blood leaking out of the gash on his temple. He blinked rapidly as some of the blood trickled into his eye. Jared struck him with the butt of the pistol again. Dustin's right cheekbone was shattered upon impact. Patches of petechiae covered his cheek while the skin around the red dots turned blue in an instant. He felt a jolt of pain in his upper gums, too.

Jared grabbed Dustin's shoulder as the young man slid down the wall. He placed the muzzle of the pistol against his neck. At point-blank range, death was guaranteed.

Patrick fell to his knees near Cody. He reached for them and shouted, "Don't! Don't! Don't! Oh God! Shoot me! Please! I lied to you! This is my fault!"

Jared snarled at Dustin, foamy saliva seeping past his gritted teeth. He wanted to shoot him, but he was worried about the noise. He tucked the gun into the back of his waistband, then he grabbed Dustin's hoodie with both hands at the chest and pulled him away from the wall. He dragged him towards the dining table.

On their way there, he kicked Patrick's head. The *whack* of his boot colliding with the side of Patrick's skull echoed through the house. Then the floorboards rattled as Patrick's face hit the floor. He was knocked unconscious by the blow. The grappling men stepped over Cody. Legs like wet noodles, Dustin nearly lost his footing every step of the way.

Dazed, Dustin muttered, "Where are you... What are you... What the..."

He caught Jared by surprise and pushed him away. Jared crashed into the dining table while Dustin bumped into a stool near the kitchen bar. He lurched towards the patio doors, but he tumbled on his way there. Some of Patrick's blood had landed in the dining area. He fell to his hands and knees near the patio doors—a meter away from his exit.

As he crawled forward, he heard a barrage of footsteps behind him. He glanced back and screamed as Jared ran towards him. He crawled faster and scrambled to his feet.

Just as Dustin was standing up, Jared grabbed the back of his hoodie with both hands. He thrust him at the patio doors—*head-first.* The glass door shattered, but none of the neighbors noticed. They were too far. Most of them had already left to the big party at Oro Center, too. Kids walked past their house at dusk with their parents, but they obeyed the sign on the door.

No candy, sorry! Do not disturb!

A cool breeze caressed Dustin's sweaty, bloody head. A large shard of glass tore his scalp open and protruded from his head. A piece of his scalp drooped over his forehead. The white of his skull was visible in the massive gash. Blood dripped from the wound and the ends of his hair, *plopping* on the ground. Other shards stabbed his forehead and cheeks, sparkling with the moonlight. Some glass fragments landed in his left eye. His eyeball and eyelids turned blood-red. He felt a stinging pain across his head, but he felt *nothing* inside of his skull, as if his brain were removed.

Yet, he managed to stay conscious.

Jared pulled him back into the house. He pushed his upper body onto the kitchen bar. He slid him to the other side of the bar. The blood acted like butter, allowing him to glide easily. He stopped near the archway leading into the kitchen. He found Cody standing at the end of the entrance hall. Shock and awe were written on his face.

Cody expected Jared to save him and restrain Dustin. He didn't expect him to beat him until he was unrecognizable—until he was dragged to the edge of death.

Jared said, "Help me carry him to the sink." Cody hesitated, stammering incoherently. Jared shouted, "Now, retard!"

Cody bolted into action. He grabbed Dustin's waist while Jared wrapped his arm around his chest. They carried him into the kitchen. They threw his upper body over the sink.

Dustin mumbled, "Wha–What... did you... do... my... dad... sis–sisters... my..."

His voice trembling, Cody asked, "Do–Do you wa–want me to get the tape?"

"We're not taping him to the sink," Jared responded.

"The–Then what are we going to do? We have to get out of here and he–he can't call the cops."

"He's not going anywhere. *We're* not going anywhere until your sister gets back with the money."

Jared forced Dustin's right hand into the garbage disposal as deep as possible. Before Cody could stop him, Jared flicked the switch and turned on the garbage disposal.

Dustin was revitalized by the pain. His eyes sprung open as he shrieked. The spinning lugs broke his bones while the grinding ring tore into his skin. *Popping* and *clunking* sounds came out of the sink. He tried to pull his hand out, but it was stuck—skin and bones tangled in lugs and grooves. He felt his pinky finger snap off his hand.

Jared stood behind him and covered Dustin's mouth with his hand. Cody hopped and gasped as blood shot out of the drain.

"Shut up, bastard!" Jared shouted. "Blame your dad for this! You hear me?! It's your dad's fault you're dying tonight!"

"Don't... kill... him," Patrick said weakly. He rolled onto his back and stared at the ceiling. He heard his son's muffled cries and the struggling garbage disposal. He cried, "I'm sorry... I love you, Dustin..."

"Turn it off!" Jared shouted as Dustin writhed in his arms. Cody didn't move. Jared yelled, "You're useless!"

He leaned forward and flicked the switch again. He grabbed Dustin's forearm, then he gave it a tug. Dustin screamed and stomped. Jared placed his boot on the counter, tightened his grip on Dustin's forearm, then he pulled again. Dustin's hand plopped out. His fingertips were shaved down to his distal interphalangeal joints. His pinky was severed, his ring finger was cut in half, and his index finger was bent back. His hand was covered in dozens of gashes and drenched in blood.

Dustin stared at his shaking hand, which looked like a bloody nub in his blurred vision, then he glanced back at Jared. He fell unconscious in the trespasser's arms. Jared dragged him out of the kitchen. As he walked past him, Patrick reached for Jared's leg and then Dustin's. He missed them by a finger. He spotted Dustin's mangled hand—*like father, like son.* But, from below, his unconscious son looked dead already. He closed his eyes and whimpered, defeated.

Jared dragged Dustin into the bathroom. He dropped him in front of the toilet. He lifted his upper body from the ground, then he dunked his head into the toilet bowl. The water splashed and sloshed and bubbled. Cody made his way to the restroom. He tiptoed over the trails of blood on the floor and he lunged over Patrick. He recognized the sounds coming from the restroom. He had his fair share of swirlies at his high school.

He stopped in the doorway leading into the bathroom. He watched as Jared drowned Dustin in the toilet. Jared gripped a fistful of Dustin's hair in one hand and the nape of his neck in the other. A *shredding* sound joined the sound of sloshing water as he widened the wound on Dustin's scalp. Plumes of blood billowed away from his face until all of the water was red. Shards of glass floated in the bloody water. His arms hit the bathtub and the sink beside the toilet while his feet slid across the smooth floor.

"You're killing him," Cody whispered.

He saw the pistol in Jared's waistband. He imagined himself running into the bathroom, taking the gun, and shooting Jared as many times as possible at point-blank range. Doubt and fear stopped him from moving.

"I can't do it," he whispered.

Dustin stopped moving after three minutes. Jared kept his head submerged underwater for two more minutes. By then, he nearly scalped Dustin with his grip on his hair. He pulled Dustin's head out of the water, but he wasn't finished yet. He placed his neck on the rim of the toilet bowl. Dustin's eyes were closed, lips pale, face lacerated, and chest motionless. The bloody water dripped from his face.

Jared lifted his knee up to his stomach, then he stomped on the back of Dustin's head. Cody closed his eyes and flinched. Upon impact, Dustin's neck was crushed and his spine was snapped by the rim of the toilet bowl and the stomping. He slid off the toilet, lifeless. The back of his head hit the bathtub. There was a large indentation on his neck where his throat was pushed in.

Jared spit at his face, then he said, "You shouldn't have come home, you rat."

He stopped as he turned to leave. Cody stood in the doorway, shaking and crying. Tears rolled down his cheeks and his lips trembled.

"No one... was supposed to die," Cody said.

"Yeah, and you were supposed to be keeping a

lookout. So, whose fault is it? Huh?"

"You said no one was going to die. You said I was just supposed to stab one person and the gun would scare them. You said–"

"Wait, shut up."

"It was supposed to be simple!"

"Shut up! Listen!"

Cody cocked his head to the side and listened. He heard the sound of blood *plopping* and a whimper in a bedroom. He opened his mouth to scream again, but then he heard it.

It was a creaking floorboard.

Jared said, "The old man. Get him before he gets out!"

Cody glanced over at the living room. Patrick was gone. Before he could move an inch, Jared jostled his way past him. Cody crashed into the door behind him, then he teetered down the hall and followed Jared. Jared grabbed the machete without stopping his brisk jog. He turned the corner and found Patrick near the front door.

Patrick fell against the door and shouted, "Help! They're killing us!" He turned the doorknob and leaned back. The door opened an inch and then another. He shouted, "God, help–"

Jared swung the machete at Patrick's popliteal fossa—*his kneepit,* the spot behind his knee. He severed his tendons, cut through his veins, and scraped his bones. A geyser of blood jetted out as Patrick staggered and screamed. Jared kicked the door shut, then he swung the machete at Patrick's other popliteal fossa. Patrick's legs gave out, launching him to the floor. He brought a neighboring console table down with him.

Jared chopped at Patrick's knees with the machete. Each chop was accompanied by a loud *thud* and a bloodcurdling shriek. Patrick's instincts led his hands to his knees to protect himself. So, Jared chopped at his hands and forearms instead. He severed Patrick's right index finger with one swing. With a diagonal chop, he almost cut his thumb off— all the way down to his wrist. By the end of the attack, both of Patrick's hands were mutilated and his legs were barely attached at the knees, hanging onto his body by tendons and arteries.

Barely conscious, Patrick coughed and mumbled, "Ho–How... co–could you... do–do... this? We were..."

Jared hooked his arms under Patrick's armpits. He dragged him back to the living room. He pushed the coffee table away with his foot, then he pushed Patrick's body up against the bottom of the sofa, forcing him to sit up on the floor. Cody felt like he was starring in a horror movie, but he didn't know the script. Survival was his only concern now. He ran to the front door and peeked out the peephole. He saw a car make a U-turn in front of the house.

"I can't go out there," he whispered. "Not like this, not right now."

He locked the door, then he peeked out the peephole again. The cul-de-sac was empty, but he couldn't take the risk. He went back to the living room. He stopped in his tracks as he spotted Jared and Patrick. Jared crouched in front of Patrick, rusty bolt-cutters in his hands. Patrick's penis and scrotum stuck out of the fly of his jeans, surrounded by wiry pubic hair. The bolt-cutters were open over his right testicle.

Cody stuttered, "D–D–Don't–"

Jared closed the bolt-cutters. The blades tore Patrick's scrotum open and ruptured his testicle. The parenchyma oozed out of the wound. It looked like rubbery spaghetti covered in blood spilling out of a cracked egg. Patrick gasped. He looked down at himself with wide, bulging eyes. The stomach-churning pain muted him. He looked at Jared, who grinned at him, and then at Cody. He couldn't withstand the pain. He fainted and fell to his side.

Cody winced and stepped back. He blacked out for a split-second. He opened his eyes to a squint, curious but terrified. Jared approached him, bolt-cutters in hand. They stared at each other for a minute. After the brutal brawl—written with musical notes of shattered glass and scuffed furniture, torn skin and broken bones, desperate cries and operatic bellows—the house was swallowed by an ominous silence.

Jared said, "We're fucking up. We need the money. *Now*. Ask your sister if she's close."

"I–I don't have the phone."

"Where is it?"

Cody shrugged while his bottom lip quivered, as if he were about to cry. Jared slapped him, then he pushed him up against the wall.

"You're telling me you lost the phone?" Jared asked. "It was your only job, retard. Your sister could have been caught already. We could be wasting our time or sitting in a fucking trap with our thumbs up our asses."

"I–I–I… We–we were–"

"Find the phone!"

Jared slammed him against the wall again, then he returned to the center of the living room and searched for the phone. Cody stood there for ten seconds, face twitching uncontrollably, then he bolted into action. He ran to the entrance hall and checked the console table—*nothing.* He went to the kitchen and scanned the countertops—*nothing.*

He hopped in place and muttered, "Fuck, fuck, fuck..."

Chapter Fifteen

Betrayal

"What did you do?" Crystal murmured as she stared out the passenger window, face smeared with blood and vomit.

She spent most of her teenage years surrounded by crime. She was trained to spot unmarked police vehicles—the emergency lights on the grille and dashboard, the spotlights on the driver's side, the mobile data terminals installed on the modified center consoles, the tinted windows. She spotted several unmarked police vehicles in Shannon's neighborhood. Some of the vehicles were empty, others were filled with scheming figures. The police were surveilling the neighborhood in a massive but covert operation.

The jig was up.

Crystal glared at Shannon and said, "Turn around, bitch."

"What? What's wrong, hun?"

"Don't play stupid with me! There are cops everywhere!"

"Wha–What are you talking about? I don't see anyone. Please, calm down. Don't let them hurt my–"

"Shut up and turn this car around before I tell them to kill *everyone* in your house! My boyfriend, he's not scared of hurting your kids. He'll hurt them *so* bad you won't even recognize them when he's done."

Shannon could see her home at the end of the cul-de-sac. It was a speck in her windshield, but she was so close. A thirty-second drive would have landed her in her driveway. A few honks would have alerted the police. But she couldn't risk her family's safety. If she had known about their suffering, she would have driven her SUV through the front door.

She made the U-turn and drove away from her neighborhood. She glanced at the rearview and sideview mirrors, searching for a sign of life or hope.

Crystal held the cell phone up to her ear, then she pressed the knife against Shannon's ribcage. She was prepared to stab her at the first sign of trouble. She didn't hear anything on the phone. It had been silent since the other trespassers first muted the call. She couldn't play stupid anymore.

She said, "Jared, I need you to answer me right now. Look out the window and look around you. There are cops everywhere. I don't know how, but... she did something. We're fucked."

"I didn't do any–"

"Shut up! Stop talking, you... you... you cunt!"

"Oh my God, I'm sorry," Shannon cried. The car swerved as her arms trembled. Makeup smeared by her tears, she begged, "Please don't hurt my family. We never hurt anyone."

"Shut up! Damn it, what is wrong with you?!"

Crystal poked her ribs with the knife. She didn't cut through her costume, but she used enough pressure to make her flinch. The SUV swerved again.

"They're onto us," Crystal said. "Get out of the house. Maybe you can sneak out through the back or something. Leave the bag, the money, the jewelry... Just leave everything and get out. Hello? Can you hear me?"

"Please tell me my family's okay."

Crystal lowered the phone and said, "If you say another word, I *will* stab you and I *will* tell them to kill your kids. I'm not playing anymore." Shannon stopped at a red light and broke down, hands over her face. Speaking at the phone, Crystal said, "Cody, brat, little bro... I know you can hear me. Get away from the house. Forget about me and Jared. You can get through this on your own. Okay? Are you there?"

The call was silent. She sighed in disappointment and looked out the rear window. She thought about her little brother. She remembered the good days and the bad days. Cody always helped her, but she couldn't help him. She thought of herself as a disappointment to her brother.

She muttered, "Oh fuck. What did we do?"

As she drove, Shannon said, "*You* haven't hurt anyone. Not yet. If you let me pull over, they'll go easy on you. You–You'll spend a few weeks at a rehabilitation center. It'll be good for you, right? I'll even vouch for you and your brother. This is... We can fix this, okay? It doesn't have to end this way, hun. Please."

Maybe she's right, Crystal thought. *Or maybe they already got away. Maybe they abandoned me. Maybe they've been using me as bait. Maybe, maybe, maybe.*

"Fuck! Goddammit!" Crystal yelled. She slammed the phone on the dashboard. She shouted, "Why did I trust him?! Why did I go through with this?! I'm so fucking stupid! Okay, okay... I still have some–some options, don't I? Yeah, I can... I can get away."

"You can–"

"Don't talk to me," Crystal interrupted. "Let me think about this for a second. They're either there or they're not. But the police are all there, so... they know something. Yeah, they're still home. I'm here. I have the money. I have the car. I can... I can leave this city... by myself. Then, I just... I'd just have to take care of myself..."

She stared at Shannon's lap as she thought about abandoning her boyfriend and her brother. It was dishonorable, she would have been betraying her brother, but it was the safest plan. She looked at Shannon. She saw her lips moving, but she didn't hear a thing. She closed her eyes and shook her head. Upon opening her eyes, she heard everything.

Eyes glimmering with hope, Shannon said, "The phone, hun. Answer the phone."

Crystal looked at the phone in her hand. The screen was cracked, but she heard a voice from the speaker. She sniffled as she raised the phone to her ear.

Cody said, "*Crystal!* Hey, can you hear me? Please say something. What happened to you? Where are you?"

"Cody? Oh, shit, Cody!" Crystal responded. "What did you do? I couldn't hear you for... fuck, for a while."

Cody stood in the living room. His palm on his forehead, he watched as Jared pummeled Patrick's face. While attempting to get help, Patrick had grabbed the phone and hid it in his pocket. He couldn't operate the phone due to his mangled hands, so he didn't bother to even attempt to call 911. His face was blue and red, bruised and bloody. His cheeks and forehead inflated like balloons.

Cody glanced over at the hallway. Images of Jill and Kimberly, heads covered in bloody pillowcases, flashed in his mind. He puffed a trembling sigh.

Teary-eyed, he said, "We fucked up, Crystal. Things, um… We went too far. Everything's… Holy shit, the–there's blood everywhere. Ja–Jared, he–he ki–"

"Are you okay?" Crystal interrupted. "That's all that matters right now, brat. Are you okay? You're not hurt, are you?"

"I–I'm not, um… I'm okay, I guess," Cody croaked out. "I'm just… This is so fucked up. I don't know if I can keep going."

"Don't say that. You have to keep going. Listen, Cody… the cops are there already. They're outside of the house. They're watching you. I don't know what they're waiting for, but they're there. You have to leave as soon as possible."

"The… cops?"

Jared stopped punching Patrick. Out of breath, he glared at Cody. *Cops*—that word was forbidden in his vocabulary, especially during ongoing crimes. He took the phone out of Cody's hand. Cody leaned back against the wall and stared vacantly at Patrick. The look in his eyes said: *my life is over.*

"Cops? What are you talking about, Crystal?" Jared asked.

"Jared… I don't know what happened, but they're coming for you. I saw them all over the cul-de-sac. I don't know if they're going to raid the house or… or call you and try to negotiate or… I have no idea what's happening or what happened."

"Are you fucking kidding me? You were supposed

to watch her. You were supposed to warn us. What the hell were you doing?!"

"I tried telling you, but you didn't answer me," Crystal hissed. "*You* were fucking around over there while *I* did all of the work out here. This is *not* my fault, asshole. What did you do to them?"

"Oh my God," Shannon cried.

Pacing in front of Cody, Jared said, "It doesn't matter. Do you have the money?"

Crystal looked at the thick envelope on the dashboard. If she were in a cartoon, dollar signs would have tattooed her eyes.

She said, "I have the money."

"Then bring it back and we'll talk about what we can do to get out of this. I'm sure there's a way. I've gotten away from these pigs before. Yeah, we can still do this..."

"Yeah, um... Yeah, I hear you."

Crystal heard him, but she stopped listening. She stared at the envelope and thought about her life—her past, her present, her future. When she thought about the past, she was reminded of her father. Jared and John Cox were very similar—mean, abusive, *destructive.* When she thought about the present, she pictured her younger brother and a house flooded with blood. And when she thought about the future, she imagined herself spending a lifetime in prison.

But why should I?–she thought.

She grabbed the envelope and held it close to her stomach. Interrupting Jared's rambling, she said, "Jared, baby, I'm going home."

"What?" Jared asked. He stopped pacing in front of Cody. The young men locked eyes. He asked, "What do you mean you're going home?"

"If I go back to the house, I'd be walking into a trap. We'd literally be driving to a dead-end. You are... You're fucked."

"Hey, Crystal, what are you saying? You have the money. It's *our* money. Your brother is right here in front of me. He's scared and he needs you. Don't do anything stupid, girl."

Her voice raspy from all her crying, Crystal said, "Tell him that I'm sorry and I love him... and I hope he'll get out of this and start a better life without a terrible sister like me."

"Don't, Crystal! Don't you fucking dare! I will find you and I'll–"

"Goodbye and good luck."

"Kill you!" Jared finished his sentence.

Crystal ended the call. She threw the phone out the window. It *clacked* as it bounced and rolled across the ground.

She pressed the knife against Shannon's ribcage and said, "Park."

"Park?"

"Park on the side of the road, leave the keys, and get out. If you don't, I'll stab you."

Shannon slowed down, but she didn't stop. Her face spasmed while her head twitched. She drove past a stop sign. Another driver stomped on his brakes and honked at her at the intersection, barely avoiding a nasty collision.

"What do you think you're doing?" Crystal asked as she poked Shannon's ribs with the knife. "You think I'm playing? You think I've never stabbed someone before?"

"I can't get out," Shannon said, eyes on the road. "You promised me my family would be okay if I followed your directions. You promised!"

"They're fine! And you lied! You told the cops!"

"They're not okay! My babies are *not* okay! I can feel it! I can see it in your eyes! What did they do to my family?!"

"The sooner you get out of the car, the sooner you can find out."

Shannon shook her head and said, "No. You're lying. I can drive home faster than I can walk. You get out of the car and you walk out of this town! I'm not abandoning my family!"

"You stupid bitch," Crystal said. "I'm just trying to survive. Why are you making this so complicated?!"

"Because I love my family!"

Red and blue lights reflected on the rearview and sideview mirrors. A police cruiser followed them from the cul-de-sac. Shannon's erratic driving and failure to stop at the stop sign gave the officer a reason to pull them over. Crystal saw red and blue flames in the mirrors—a wave of fire rolling towards them. Her plan—*her world*—was burning. She was consumed by her rage.

She thrust the knife into Shannon's ribcage—one, two, three, *four times.* She stabbed her upper arm once, tearing her bicep open, and she cut into her stomach twice. During the stabbing, the blade punctured one of her lungs and cracked two ribs. Shannon tightened her grip on the steering wheel as she shrieked. She inadvertently stomped on the gas pedal while swerving in and out of her lane.

Forty. Fifty. Sixty. Seventy miles per hour.

And only ten seconds had passed since the stabbing began.

"Stop!" Shannon cried out as she pushed Crystal away. "What are you–"

The SUV crashed into the driver's side of a sedan at an intersection. The sound of clunking metal, shattering glass, and screeching wheels exploded through the area. The sedan spun in circles at the intersection until the passenger side collided with a traffic light pole. The SUV glided towards a gas station at the opposite corner. The edge of the passenger side wheels hit the sidewalk. The vehicle flipped into the parking lot. It rolled four times, then it landed on its wheels beside a gas pump.

"Oh my God!" a woman yelled from the gas station. She ran back into the store and watched the aftermath of the crash from the storefront windows. Muffled but audible, she repeated, "Oh my God! Oh my God!"

Crystal groaned as she awoke. She heard a buzzing sound. Half of her vision was blurred and red. She couldn't see out of her other eye. After five seconds, she grimaced and screamed as pain surged from *every* part of her body.

She faced Shannon before the crash, her side against the back of her seat. The airbag deployed and *snapped* her right arm at the elbow in front of her. The bone stuck out of the crook of her elbow and cut through the sleeve of her hoodie while her forearm and hand pointed to her right at a forty-five-degree angle. Her left leg was broken—a shattered kneecap, a broken tibia, and a twisted ankle. Her foot pointed *behind* her.

All of the windows were shattered. Glass filled the interior of the car. Shards stuck out of her face, neck, and hands. Smaller glass particles dusted her shoulders and jeans. Her right eye was crushed by the airbag and mutilated by the glass. She couldn't open it. Blood seeped past her eyelids and waterfalled out of her eye socket. Her orange wig was painted red by the blood gushing out of the gash on the back of her head. A large, crooked gash stretched across the bridge of her nose. Several of her ribs were cracked and her sternum was broken. Each breath was painful.

After a minute, she heard the emergency sirens surrounding the scene of the accident. Through the broken mirror, she saw a figure approaching the wrecked sedan. Her vision focused.

A cop spoke to the driver of the sedan, but she couldn't hear his words. The cop staggered back as the driver's door popped open halfway. The driver—a red-haired woman in her forties—appeared to be attached to the door. The door was pushed inward during the collision. The top of the door was bent. As the car hit the pole, the driver was flung to the right and then back to the left. The top of the door penetrated her head at the temple. The door nearly severed the top half of her head.

The passenger of the vehicle moaned and squirmed in her seat, trapped by her seatbelt, the airbag, and the pole beside her. She was crying for her mother. Her wounds weren't visible from the SUV, but her pain—her heartache—could be heard throughout the city. She was devastated by the crash, physically and emotionally. During a regular drive home, her life changed forever because of another driver. Life was cruel and mysterious.

"Oh!" Crystal gasped as she turned her attention to Shannon, who was slumped back in her seat.

Shannon's airbag deployed, but it was instantly ruptured by a large shard of the windshield. And that large shard struck Shannon's face with enough force to penetrate her skull. From her scalp to the bridge of her nose, her face was split open. Through the blood and glass, pieces of her skull and brain were visible in the massive gash. One eye was open, wide and bloodshot, while the other was open halfway. Blood cascaded across her face. Her death was instantaneous.

"Sh–Shit," Crystal stuttered as she wiggled between her seat and the airbag.

She gasped and whimpered as she reached for the pocket-knife on the center console with her free hand. Twinges rocketed through her body with the slightest movements. She exhaled loudly as she finally grabbed the knife. She gritted her teeth and thrust it at the airbag. The sound of the airbag bursting—a pop and a long, loud hiss—echoed through the street. She found the bloody envelope on her lap. She didn't have the time or the energy to open it and count the cash.

"Oh fuck," she cried as she glanced out the rear window.

The officer approached the SUV, one hand on his holster and the other on his chest-mounted radio. He reported the activity in the SUV to his dispatcher. More wailing sirens rapidly approached the accident.

Saliva spurting from her clenched teeth, Crystal

fought through the pain and reached for her seatbelt. She unbuckled it. She yelped as it hit her broken arm on the way back to its regular position. The door was locked before the accident, but it was now unlocked and open. She pushed it with her shoulder. She screamed again as she climbed out of the SUV, bouncing on her only good foot. She held the knife in her left hand while clenching the envelope close to her stomach.

As he approached, the officer said, "Ma'am, don't move. You were in an accident. I need you to sit down. Can you do that for me?"

"Sta–Stay a–away from me."

"Ma'am, please. You're injured. An ambulance is on the way. Take a seat."

"I can't... I–I'm *not* going to jail."

"No one said anything about jail. You need..."

The officer stopped as he spotted the knife in her hand. He drew his handgun, but he aimed it at the ground. He sidestepped to his left, maneuvering himself so he wouldn't accidentally shoot at the gas pump or at the customers in the gas station.

He said, "Drop the knife. Come on, don't do this."

Crystal staggered about, struggling to keep her broken leg from hitting the floor. She felt like the ground was tilting under her. She hopped forward, hissing and whimpering in pain. Tears flooded her good eye and blurred her vision again. She saw the outline of the officer's body—a shadowy figure illuminated from behind by a streetlamp. The cop stood five meters away, but, in her distorted vision, he looked like he was across the street.

Startled but prepared, the cop aimed at her

stomach and stepped back as Crystal limped forward. The envelope fell to the ground.

Crystal swung the knife in his direction and shouted, "It's mine!"

"Don't do that!" the cop barked as he took another step back. "Get on the ground! Now!"

"Fuck you! Fuck every single one of you!"

She swung the knife again. She lost her balance and lurched towards the cop. She screamed with each step she took with her broken foot. To the cop, it sounded like a battle cry. He shot at her twice. One bullet entered her abdomen, went through her intestines, and exited through the small of her back. The second bullet entered her ribcage, punctured one of her lungs, and then was caught in one of her ribs.

She collapsed in front of the officer. The cop reported the shooting to his dispatcher as he kicked the knife away from her.

Still aiming the gun at her, he demanded, "Roll over! Get on your stomach!"

Crystal didn't hear him. She was deafened by the pain. Instead, she curled into the fetal position. Her head bobbed, her limbs twitched, and her entire body shuddered. Her blood was hot and plentiful, but she felt cold. She felt as if all of the blood were siphoned from her veins and replaced with ice. Her heartbeat slowed to three seconds between each beat—then four, *then five.*

She stared at the bloody envelope. She reached for it, but it was too far. Her limp arm hit the floor. She closed her good eye.

"Give... it... to... my brother," she said weakly.

She let out one last exhale, then she stopped breathing. Her body continued to twitch for a minute while the police surrounded her and a small audience of customers recorded the event with their cell phones from the gas station.

Chapter Sixteen

Trouble in Paradise

"Goddammit!" Jared shouted.

He threw the cell phone at the television. The screens cracked. The TV was slanted on its wall mount. He kicked the recliner, then he flipped the coffee table. He looked to his right, then to his left. He searched for something—*or someone*—to punch. He struck Patrick with an uppercut, and then two more. He shattered Patrick's nose and chipped some of his incisors.

The blood on his face covered Patrick's thin smile. He was devastated by the death and violence, but he found some joy in Jared's fear and panic.

"What happened?" Cody asked, eyes dull and glazed with tears.

"Your sister, that fucking bitch, is running with our money!"

"You... Are you sure?"

Jared stomped on Patrick's chest. The kick made a *splat* sound due to the blood soaked into the costume. Patrick grimaced, wheezed, and squirmed in pain.

"I'm positive!" Jared shouted as he jabbed his index finger at Cody.

Cody shook his head and said, "No, she wouldn't do something like that."

"Are you actually retarded? Huh? One more day and your sister would have sold you for crack. You'd be in Mexico or China. They'd be filling up your dead body with drugs or taking all of your organs out and selling 'em to other unlucky bastards for a pretty penny. She took the money and ran, Cody. And the cops are outside watching us. That fucking slut, we shouldn't have sent her out there..."

"It can't be true," Cody whispered as he lowered his head, ignoring Jared's rambling.

He saw his tears dripping onto the floorboard between his sneakers. He understood his sister's disease, but he always believed their bond was stronger than her addiction. They were friends as much as they were family. They took care of each other during their darkest times. Her selfishness crushed him. The only person he ever trusted turned her back on him.

"She never cared about me," he whispered.

Jared peeked out the peephole on the front door, then he looked out the kitchen window. He noticed a car parked in the cul-de-sac and a black SUV with tinted windows parked in front of a neighbor's house. He walked back to the living room. He scanned every corner until he spotted the broken patio door.

He said, "We've still got a few options, man. We can make a run for it through the back. We'd have to move fast, though, and we'd end up somewhere in the desert. Or we can take one of those cars in the garage and race them. Lead them to Oro Center and lose them in the traffic, then just drive off or... or get out and get lost in the crowds. Either way, we have a few grand in jewelry in here. We can buy our way into Mexico."

"I'm not going with you," Cody said.

"What? Then what are you going to do? Huh? Hope your sister comes back and saves your ass? I told you:

she abandoned you and she doesn't give a *fuck* about you."

"I don't care. I'm not moving. Let them catch me. Whatever. I'm done."

Jared stepped up to him and glared down at him. He said, "If you stay, if you get caught by the police... then I know you'll snitch. You'll tell them your life story *and* mine. You know what that means, right?" Cody lowered his head. Jared gave him a gentle slap, then he said, "It means I can't trust you. It means you're a loose end. I can't leave any loose ends. So, do you know what I have to do to you?"

"If you want to fight me, then fight me. It won't change anything. It's over. We lost."

Jared smirked and said, "I didn't lose a thing, Cody. And I'm not just going to fight you. That's not how you silence people." He gripped Cody's neck and slammed him against the wall. He hissed, "I'm going to kill you, you little punk. Then I'm going to kill everyone in this house. And then I'm going to hunt your sister down and slaughter her."

Cody grabbed Jared's forearm and croaked, "Don– Don't hur–hurt my–"

Jared slammed him against the wall again, then he pushed him towards the living room. Cody lurched into the dining area. He crashed into one of the chairs, then into the sofa, and then he fell to his knees. As he struggled to his feet, Jared tackled him from behind, ramming his back with his shoulder. Cody lost his balance and reeled towards the patio doors. Jared tackled him again, crushing him against the wall beside the broken door.

The glass patio door rattled, shards raining down

to the floor. The wall groaned after a loud *thud*. Some of the picture frames on the wall shook while others fell off the wall, cracking and clacking on the floorboards. Cody tried to squirm away, but Jared dug his shoulder into his back and kept him pinned to the wall. He felt a twinge in his spine—a jolt of pain running from the nape of his neck to the small of his back.

"*Ow!*" he cried out. "Stop it! Please, man! What the fuck?!"

Without moving his shoulder, Jared grabbed the back of Cody's head with his free hand. Fistful of hair, he pulled Cody's head back, then he slammed his face against the wall. The gash on Cody's bottom lip widened. His mouth and chin were covered in blood. Blotches of pink and white were visible *inside* of his busted, mushy lip. One of his lower incisor teeth was ejected from his gums. He swallowed the tooth—and he didn't notice it.

Jared shouted, "I should have never trusted any of you!"

He pulled Cody away from the wall, then he pushed him through the patio door face-first. The patio door shattered while the door beside it cracked and wobbled.

Dazed by the crash, Cody stumbled outside. He fell to one knee, stood up, teetered around for a few steps, and then fell to his knees. He stood up, only to stagger again. Shards of glass stuck out of his face and scalp. A large shard pierced his eyebrow. Some of the small glass particles sparkled in the wound in his lip, which was now numb. Patches of glass stretched across his cheeks and nose, too. Blood shot out of his scalp in geysers, but the wounds weren't visible under his hair.

He mumbled, "Wha–What hap–happened to... to you?"

He stared vacantly ahead. He saw a small pool in front of him with calm, clean water. A brick wall stood behind the pool and wrapped itself around the property. Beyond the wall, he spotted the mountains in the desert, illuminated by the dazzling stars and moon. He swore he even saw coyotes prowling the empty land, searching for food and shelter.

But he could only focus on the pool.

He saw Crystal standing *on* the pool. She wasn't standing at the bottom of the pool, she wasn't swimming or floating, and she wasn't partially submerged at the shallow end. She was standing on the surface of the water, like Jesus in the New Testament. But his sister was naked and covered in blood. He couldn't see any wounds on her, but he spotted the dim, hollow look of death in her eyes.

"What happened to you?" he repeated, teary-eyed.

His vision faded and a hollow *ping* sound echoed through the desolate cul-de-sac. He hit the ground face-first. He awoke ten seconds later. Blood rushed down to his face from a wound on the back of his head. He groaned and whimpered and hissed as he touched the wound. He rolled over onto his back. Through his blurred vision, he found Jared standing over him with an aluminum baseball bat in his hand.

Jared pointed the bat at Cody, as if he were holding a long blade, then he said, "I treated you like a brother. I gave you a chance to join us, then... then your sister betrayed us and then *you* betrayed me. It runs in the family, huh? You're just a bunch of traitors!"

He swung the bat at Cody's chest. Cody grimaced in pain and flopped on the floor. A rib snapped and his sternum cracked. He crossed his arms over his chest and wiggled on his back, inching towards the pool. Jared swung away at his arms. He broke the bones in Cody's forearms and wrists while tenderizing his muscles. Under the sleeves of Cody's hoodie, the young teenager's arms were red, blue, and purple.

Jared swung the bat at Cody's stomach. The blow knocked the air out of him. Jared struck him again before he could cover his stomach. Cody felt something *pop* inside of him. Then a horrifying warmth spread across his abdominal cavity—*internal bleeding.* He panted and wheezed as he writhed in pain. He entered a state of panic.

Barely audible, he stammered, "I-I-I d-d-don't wa-want to-to d-die."

Jared swung the bat at his face. The end cap of the baseball bat struck Cody's chin. Another tooth flew out of his gums and rolled down into his throat, like a ring slipping off a finger and down a drain. The impact of the blow left a vertical gash from his bottom lip to his jawline. The cut on his lip looked like it was connected to the gash on his chin, creating a large, bloody 'T.' He was knocked unconscious.

"I was trying to help you!" Jared shouted. "You came to me! You begged *me* to help you! And I was going to take you with me. I was going to help you until the very end. But I get it now. You and your sister come from *trash.* Your family is pathetic. Poor, stupid, sick, weak... pathetic... junkies! Bastards! Cunts! Why did I ever trust you?!"

He grabbed the hood of Cody's sweater and dragged him to the edge of the pool. Cody awoke to a view of the night sky. Due to the blood in his eyes, the stars twinkled with a red glow. There was only one question in his mind: *what happened?* He couldn't remember the minutes before he was knocked out, as if the attack had knocked those memories out of his head.

He mumbled, "Crys-Crystal, sh-she needs..."

Jared rolled him onto his stomach. He sat on Cody's back, grabbed another fistful of his hair, and then dunked his head into the pool. Underwater, Cody immediately unleashed his last breath. The water bubbled around his head, then it sloshed and splashed. His blood billowed away from him, creating red clouds around him. He kicked, he flopped, but he couldn't pull his head out of the pool.

Let go, his inner voice said. *It's over. It's not worth it. None of this was ever worth it. Better off dead, better off dead. Die!*

He stopped resisting. One of his hands fell into the pool, limp. Jared sat on him and kept his head underwater for another fifteen seconds. Then he stood up and spat on the back of Cody's head.

He stomped and shouted, "Damn it! We had a deal! We could have gotten out of this alive, retard! What the fuck am I going to do now? What am I supposed-"

Jared stopped as soon as he spotted the grill near the patio door. Some utensils sat on the grill's tray: a spatula, tongs, a meat thermometer, a brush, and a chimney starter. Beside the grill, there was a bag of charcoal and a bottle of lighter fluid. An idea popped into his head. He rushed into the house, leaving Cody near the pool.

In the living room, Patrick mumbled indistinctly. He wanted to insult Jared: *trouble in paradise, eh?* But he couldn't speak. He wiggled on the floor in front of the sofa.

Jared made his way to the garage. He ignored the cars and instead scanned the storage locker and the workbench. His eyes stopped on a red gasoline container in the corner of the room. He smirked. A fire burned in his eyes.

***

Outside, plainclothes police officers swarmed the cul-de-sac. Some stood on the sidewalks while others found shelter in their vehicles. They communicated through their radios, discussing the ongoing situation while planning a raid on the house. They waited for the SWAT team to suit up and arrive. They heard some noise from the house—shattering glass, *pings* from the baseball bat, loud grunting and fierce shouting—but it wasn't enough to alarm them because they didn't hear any feminine shrieks.

If Kimberly or Jill screamed, they would have felt compelled to enter the house without reinforcements. The girls' safety was their primary concern.

In the meantime, they waited in silence and continued to surveil the area. The news of the deadly car crash reached them just as Jared beat Cody in the patio of the Cohen house.

Chapter Seventeen

Another Playdate

Jared entered the master bedroom with the gasoline container. He poured some gasoline on the clothes in the closet, the bed, the curtains, and the dresser—just enough to help the fire spread. He splashed some more gasoline on the floor and walls in the hallway. He went into Kimberly's room. She was still taped to the bed, although the duct tape was tearing. Her torn underwear was crumpled near her feet and the crotch of her dress was blotted with blood.

"Hey, baby," Jared said as he walked into the room. Kimberly let out a ghastly groan under her pillowcase. Jared said, "It looks like it's time for me to go. I wish I could take you with me. Vegas, Mexico… They're not places for kids like you. Besides, you'd draw too much attention to us. It just wouldn't work out. I really wish it didn't have to end this way. You can blame your mom and that *bitch* I sent out with her. Blame your daddy, too, 'cause he couldn't save you. No one can save you."

Kimberly whimpered as gasoline hit her costume and the pillowcase over her head. The strong scent caused her head to hurt. Jared didn't *soak* her in gasoline because he needed enough to cover the house. He figured a few drops was enough to set her aflame as soon as the fire started. And if the fire didn't kill her, he hoped smoke inhalation would finish the job. He splashed some gasoline on her bed and some of the other furniture, then he went to Jill's room.

Kimberly moaned as she tried to pull her arms away from the bedpost. Centimeter-by-centimeter, the tear on the tape stretched. Her mind was foggy, she felt like she was lost in a maze, but she was determined to escape. Thoughts of her family motivated her. She remembered them before the home invasion—before the mutilations, before the drugs, *before the pain.* The floorboards screeched as the bed moved, but it went unnoticed.

Jared towered over Jill. He ran his eyes over her body. He stopped at her bare crotch and smirked. Jill stared back at him, eyes cracked open to narrow slits. *A clown with a gas container*—she didn't recognize him.

"Who are you?" she asked weakly. "Where... Where's my sister?"

"I took care of her."

"What... did... you do?"

"I told you: I took care of her. She's safe."

"Really? Good... That's good."

Jared licked his lips as he leered at her crotch. He sighed and shook his head. *Don't do it,* he told himself, *you don't have time for that.* He poured gasoline on the bed, the desk, and the vanity table. He approached her again. He held the gasoline container over her body, but he couldn't dump the gasoline on her. He found himself gazing at her crotch again.

"Shit," he muttered. "Just one nut before I go. Just one."

"What are you–"

Jared fell to his knees in front of her. He grabbed her thighs and pulled her closer to him. She yelped, then she groaned and sobbed. She was familiar with rape thanks to Cody's disturbed actions earlier in the night. *It's happening again,* she thought as tears raced down her cheeks, *why does this keep happening to me?!*

Jared's fingers twitched with excitement as he struggled to unbuckle his pants. His erect penis flopped out. Pre-ejaculate glistened on his glans. He was ready. There wasn't an ounce of fear in his blood. He had been in that position before, and it aroused him. He grabbed her thighs again, lifted her from the floor, and repositioned himself.

"God!" he gasped as he thrust into her. "Damn, you're so tight, baby. That's why... he cummed... so fast."

"No," Jill cried.

She placed one foot on his leg and the other on his lower abdomen. She tried to kick him off, but she was too weak to overpower him. Her feet slid off him and her legs hit the floor.

"Stop," she said. "Please... stop it. Don't... Please..."

Jared slid his palms across her back, then he squeezed her shoulders and accelerated his thrusting. The bed moved with each thrust, headboard banging against the wall. He rubbed his cheek against hers, then he kissed her jaw and her neck. He slowed down after a minute. He didn't want to ejaculate yet. With his palms planted on the floor, he leaned away from Jill and gazed into her heavy-lidded eyes.

He asked, "You like that? Huh? Does it feel good? Tell me how much you love it. You love daddy's dick, don't you?"

Daddy—Jill grimaced upon hearing that word. The

memories came flooding in. She remembered every detail of the violent attack.

The blood.

So much blood.

"Daddy!" she cried out with a raspy, cracking voice.

Jared pulled his hips back until only the glans penetrated her, then he thrust it all into her. He repeated the process, trying his best to pound her cervix with his cock. Her whimpers and her squealing, her weeping and her pleading, made him more violent. He growled as he raped her. He wasn't a regular, flawed man. He was a beast wearing a suit of human skin—a wolf in sheep's clothing.

"No," Patrick said from the living room. His voice was weak, but he was loud enough to reach them. Laying on his side, too afraid to move, he said, "Leave her... alone."

Jared slowed his thrusting. Jill's vagina *squelched* thanks to his pre-ejaculate. She wasn't producing any arousal fluid during the violent attack. She twitched and groaned due to the pain and anxiety swelling in her body. She stared at the ceiling and tried to block out the rape. She counted each passing second, but it wouldn't end.

How long has it been? Minutes? Hours? Days?

Jared said, "I'm tired of your old man. I bet you're tired of him, too. Well, he must be lonely out there, so let's pay him a little visit?"

He tore the tape around her wrists and the bedpost with his teeth and hands. Jill slapped his cheek as soon as she was freed from her restraints. But the slap was so weak that he didn't even feel it. Jared grabbed her ankles and dragged her out of the room. Jill grabbed the doorframe. Her fingers slid off with one tug of her ankles. Some of her hair fell into a gap between the floorboards. With another tug, the hair was torn off her scalp. It stuck out of the floorboards like weeds from a sidewalk.

He released her ankles and allowed her legs to hit the floor on the opposite side of the coffee table from Patrick. Through his foggy, dim vision, Patrick saw his partially-nude daughter from under the table. After an hour of torment and uncertainty, they finally locked eyes. Despite the blood—the gore, *the mutilation*—they found some relief and comfort in each other's presence. Patrick reached for her under the table. Jill did the same. Their fingertips were inches apart, like God's and Adam's in *The Creation of Adam*.

But this was *The Destruction of the Cohens.*

Before they could touch, Jared fell to his knees in front of Jill. He leaned over and penetrated her again. He raped her in front of her father.

"No! No! No!" Patrick shouted, bloody sputum hanging from his mouth.

Jill shook and cried, "Dad... Dad..."

"No! God, leave her alone!"

Jared glared at him from under the table. While thrusting into Jill, he barked, "I told you not to fuck with me! I warned you! This could have been easy! So! Fucking! Easy!" He sped up his thrusting, moving as fast as possible. He growled, then he screamed, and then he yelled, "This is what you get for cheating me! Blame your whore wife! Blame yourself! Goddammit!"

His penis slipped out of her. In a rush, he rubbed it

against her labia. It slid downward. He pushed it up, then he forced it into her anus. He wasn't trying to sodomize her, but he didn't care. He noticed the difference between vaginal sex and anal sex, but *he did not care.*

Jill shrieked in three blurts—*ahh! Ahh! Ahh!* She convulsed as pain shot out from her pelvis and spread across her body. She felt like she was being impaled. Jared slapped his hand over her mouth. Her muffled shrieks were barely loud enough to reach the front yard. Her eyes rolled back and she breathed deeply through her nose.

Grunting between each word, each thrust, Jared said, "You... like it... don't you? You've.... You've done it... before... haven't you? You slut... You rich... dirty... fucking slut!"

"Dad," she gasped. The pain smothered her voice. She stuttered, "He-Help me. Pl-Please, d-dad, d-don't let-"

"Shut up!" Jared roared as he punched her face. His gloved knuckles cut her chin. He hit her a second and then a third time. He shouted, "You bitch! Take this dick! *Take it!*"

He growled as he thrust his penis into her ass, forcing it in until her thighs touched his hips. He clenched his ass, he grunted, and he moaned as he ejaculated inside of her.

Teeth chattering, Patrick asked, "What did you do?" He looked at his daughter, who was barely conscious. He sniffled and said, "Baby, sweetie, princess... You're okay. It's going... It's going to be okay. Get up and-and run. Please, baby, get out of the... Get out of this damn house! Get up! Jill, please!

Don't do this to me!"

Jared pulled out of her. Blood and semen oozed out of her widened anus. A streak of smeared feces stained the shaft of his penis, beads of blood clung to the glans, and a string of semen hung from his urethra. He grimaced in disgust, then he chuckled in amazement. He didn't bother cleaning his dick. He shoved it into his boxers and jumped up to his feet. He strolled away, as if nothing had happened.

"How could you do this to her?!" Patrick yelled as Jared walked past him. He grabbed Jared's boot, but Jared kept walking. Patrick cried, "You're a bastard! You'll burn in hell for this! I swear... *I swear*, you'll pay for this, boy. If–If you don't kill me... if the cops don't kill you... I'm going to find you and I'm going to make you suffer. Oh, boy, I'm going to hurt you!"

Jared ignored him. He approached the backpack at the other side of the room. He looked through his supplies, then he walked into the kitchen.

Patrick coughed and groaned as he dragged himself around the coffee table. His head bobbed every inch of the way, like a sleepy child's in the backseat of a car. He faded in and out, anemic due to his severe loss of blood. The pain from his ruptured testicle left him shaking. But he was determined to comfort his daughter. He felt her pain more than he felt his own. It took him five minutes to reach her.

He caressed her face with his mutilated hands, smearing his blood on her cheeks. Her eyes flickered open. She smiled upon spotting her father. His face was swollen, bloody, and bruised, but she only saw the bravest, most handsome man in the world beside her. Her superhero, the man who always promised to protect her, finally arrived.

His face twitching as he forced a smile, Patrick said, "Baby... Jill... I'm so sorry."

"It's not... your fault," Jill said with a gentle, fading voice.

Patrick said, "Hey, don't sleep. You're going to be okay. The cops are..." He paused to swallow the lump in his throat. He said, "They're outside right now. Your mom, she, um... She got help. She's saving us right now. She's amazing, isn't she?"

"Mom..."

"Yeah, mom. She's coming, baby. You want to see her, don't you?"

"Kim... Kimmy... Is Kimmy okay?"

"I–I'm going to find her and we'll–"

Patrick gasped and fell back as a machete struck Jill's neck. Jared leaned over the coffee table, holding the handle of the long, sharp blade. Jill squeezed her eyes shut and trembled. The machete ruptured her trachea and esophagus. Blood shot up into her mouth and dribbled out of her nose. More blood flooded her lungs and stomach. She tried to breathe, but she could only gag and croak.

"No!" Patrick shouted as he scrambled back to his daughter's side.

And, just as Patrick reached her, Jared pulled the blade out of her neck. Blood sprinkled out of her open throat. Patrick placed his hands over the wound. His broken, mutilated fingers shook because of the pain, but he fought through it. He tried to stop the bleeding while searching for a way to help his daughter breathe.

An incision, he thought. *I have to get the blood out*

of her lungs and I have to clear her airway.

He looked at Jared and stammered, "G–G–Get me a–a scalpel or a–a knife. She can still ma–make it. Please, kid, pl–please." Jared gave him a steady, emotionless stare. Patrick shouted, "Help us!"

Jared said, "She's gone. Blame your wife." He stared at Jill's twitching face. Her cheeks darkened to a light tint of blue and the color disappeared from her lips. Jared said, "You hear me? Blame your mom."

"No!" Patrick shouted. He leaned closer to Jill's face. Panic in his raspy voice, he said, "It's not your mom's fault. It's not your fault, either. You hear me? Don't be scared, baby. Daddy's here. I'm here, Jill. Don't... Oh God, just fight it. The police are coming. Right?! You're out there, aren't you?! Come and save us! What the fuck are you waiting for?!"

As Patrick screamed at the walls, Jared walked around the living room and doused the furniture in gasoline. Patrick wept as it rained down on him. Jill stopped breathing. The gasoline entered the wound on her neck and landed in her eyes, but she didn't react. She passed away beside her father, brutalized by a deranged intruder—her life robbed on what should have been a fun night with friends and family.

Chapter Eighteen

The Inferno

Jared splashed some gasoline on the curtains over the patio doors. He peeked outside and spotted Cody near the pool. He walked into the living room. He shook the gasoline container. He was running low on gasoline, so he examined the kitchen and searched for the most flammable objects. Patrick slid his arm under Jill's head and rubbed his cheek against her soft hair. His tears trickled down to her face as he caressed her jaw. He repeatedly apologized to her, slurring his words: *I'm so so-sorry, I'm sorry, so so-sorry.*

The sound of a groaning floorboard interrupted them. After three quiet seconds, another floorboard cried. They heard fingernails scraping the wall, too.

Jared and Patrick glanced over at the hallway. To their utter surprise, Kimberly walked with her feet wide apart into the living room with the pillowcase over her head and her arms outstretched. One hand touched the wall, the other hovered in front of her. The crotch of her dress was stained with blood on each side. Some fresh blood rolled down the back of her thighs. Like her older sister, Jared made her bleed during the sexual assault. The heroin left her dazed. She could have removed the pillowcase and the duct tape, but she wasn't thinking clearly.

She spoke indistinctly under the pillowcase, her voice muffled by the tape over her mouth. She said something along the lines of: *Mom... Dad... Where am*

I? Can you help me? Can somebody help me? Hello?

She bumped into the wall in front of her. The entrance hall was to her left while the kitchen, dining area, and living room were to her right. She was close to the exit, but she didn't realize it.

"Well, look who decided to join the party," Jared said as he approached her.

Patrick set Jill's head down gently, then he dragged himself forward. He said, "Don't... touch... her." He stopped as he reached the entrance of the hallway to the bedrooms. He said, "Please, not her. She's... She's only thirteen for crying out loud. She's a child, young man. She's an innocent, *lovely* child. You don't want to hurt her. Let her go. Let her walk out. She can't stop you. She's not a threat. Can you... Can you spare her?"

"It's funny how things change so quickly, isn't it? Just a few minutes ago, you were threatening to make me 'suffer.' Now, 'boy' changes to 'young man.' I'm not a bastard anymore, am I?"

"I'm sorry."

"I know you are. I wish I could help. I mean it. I liked the girl. She cried a lot, but she didn't fight me. She wasn't an uptight *cunt* like you. But, I don't have a lot of options here."

"Oh God."

"I can't leave any witnesses."

"No, please! She's thirteen!"

"Thirteen-year-olds die every day, man. This is life. It's fucked up, but... that's how it is."

Jared dumped the rest of the gasoline on her. The liquid soaked the pillowcase and landed on her dress. Kimberly instinctively stepped forward. She bumped into the wall in front of her head-first. Patrick crawled towards them. He forced himself onto his knees, despite the deep, grisly wounds on his kneepits. He clasped his hands in front of his chest and begged indistinctly.

Jared opened his stainless-steel lighter. A flame shot out. He held it over Kimberly's head while gazing into Patrick's bloodshot eyes. He smirked at him. He didn't care about the girl at all.

A shard of glass *cracked* and *popped.* The men looked over at the patio door, baffled by the noise.

Cody lurched into the house, blood and water dripping from his face. Jared was surprised and impressed by Cody's survival. He was so shocked that he couldn't react.

Cody tackled Jared, wrapping his arms around him while pressing his face against his chest. They bumped into Kimberly, causing her to stagger to the left, then they crashed into the wall.

"What the hell are you doing?!" Jared shouted. He swung his elbow down at Cody's back—one, two, three, four, *five times.* He yelled, "What the fuck?! Don't fuck this up! Cody, stop!"

Cody felt pain across every inch of his body, but he refused to release him. He sought vengeance and redemption. He leaned back and used all of his body weight to pull Jared away from the wall. They crashed into the archway, stumbled into the kitchen, and crashed into a counter. The open lighter fell out of Jared's hand and landed on a gasoline-soaked rag on the neighboring counter.

The rag was set aflame. The weight of the lighter pushed the burning rag off the counter. It landed on a puddle of gasoline on the floor, which ignited a trail of fire. The fire led to the wall. The curtains over the window and the patio door were set aflame. One of the burning patio door curtains fell off its rod and burned another puddle in the living room. The furniture was set aflame next.

Within a minute, a roaring fire swallowed the kitchen and living room.

Jared smashed a glass cup on the back of Cody's head. He saw the dark blood coming out of his scalp. He smashed another cup on his head. The wound widened and blood sprayed out in every direction. Yet, Cody didn't loosen his grip. He pulled Jared away from the counter, then he rammed the small of Jared's back against the countertop. Jared screamed as he felt a twinge in his spine.

Cody grabbed a knife from the knife block. He stabbed the side of Jared's torso twice, then he thrust the blade into his lower abdomen four times. He used Jared's technique to try to neutralize him without exposing his jaw to a knockout blow. Howling in pain, Jared kneed Cody in the stomach. Cody released the knife, leaving it in Jared's gut. His legs wobbled, but he stayed on his feet.

With his arms still wrapped around him, Cody pulled away from Jared, then he lunged at him. He bit into Jared's neck. His grip was weak due to his missing teeth, but he managed to penetrate his flesh. He tasted the pungent blood in his mouth. It tasted the same as his own. *He's not a monster,* he thought, *he's a normal guy, just like me.* He shook his head and sank his teeth deeper into his neck, trying his best to tear a chunk off him.

Jared hit Cody's body with one hook after

another—left, right, *left*. It was ineffective. He pulled Cody's hair, but that only helped Cody pull on Jared's neck. He heard his own skin *ripping* under the pressure. Blood cascaded down to his chest, then flowed down to join the blood around his stab wounds. The fire and the fight left him drenched in sweat and blood. He used all of the energy he could muster to push Cody back. He slammed him against the opposite countertop.

Cody's grip on Jared's neck loosened as he fought for air. He felt his flesh slipping out of his mouth. So, he dug his thumb into one of the stab wounds on Jared's stomach.

Jared shouted, "Shit! Stop!"

In a daze, Kimberly turned right and walked towards the fire in the dining area. Patrick reached for her ankle, but he missed her by a foot. He couldn't grab her with his broken fingers anyway.

He shouted, "Kimmy! This way! Over here! Baby, listen to me!"

Kimberly took another step towards the fire. Patrick looked to his left, then to his right, searching for a way to capture her attention.

He stared at her again and sang: ♪ *Oh, baby, hold me closer! Don't tell me that it's over!*

Kimberly stopped. She was surrounded by the sounds of chaos: men grunting and screaming, fire crackling and popping, glass crunching and cracking. But, despite his damaged vocal cords and the surrounding ruckus, she recognized her father's voice and her favorite song. She turned around. She stepped away from the flames and moved towards the entrance hall.

As she plodded towards the exit, she mumbled under the tape: ♪ *C–Cause I know it–it ain't over!*

Patrick said, "Oh, ba–baby, ho–hold me... me..." He broke down while singing. He swiped at the tears and sweat racing down his face, then he watched his daughter as she approached the front door. He wished he could have followed her, but he was too weak to move again. He whispered, "Cause I know it ain't over... Go, baby. *Survive.*"

Kimberly hummed the melody of the song to herself while struggling with the locks. The heat from the fire hit her back. She imagined a demon breathing down her neck. She heard a *click*. She turned the knob, pushed the door open, and stumbled onto the porch. A blanket of black smoke followed her. She felt like the cool breeze was wrapping itself around her, protecting her from the demon in the house.

"It's a girl! Don't shoot!" a man shouted from beyond the front gate.

A woman yelled, "This way! Over here, honey!"

Kimberly blinked a few times. She could only see an orange glow. She realized the pillowcase was still over her head. She removed it and blinked rapidly to clear her vision. She spotted four police officers in front of her home's front gate, aiming their pistols at the house. An officer found cover behind a brick wall to her left, his rifle aimed at the porch and his finger on the trigger.

There were more plainclothes cops in the unmarked vehicles in the neighborhood. Red and blue lights cycled from a police cruiser parked at the center of the cul-de-sac.

She took the tape off her mouth and cried, "Mom!

Mom! I–I want my mommy!"

The female officer crouched her way to the patio. She peeked into the house through the open front door. She saw the fire in the dining area as well as Patrick's body. From the outside looking in, he looked dead. She helped Kimberly climb onto her back, then she raced back to the front gate with the injured girl while her partners protected her from behind their cover. Kimberly looked back at the burning house, awe written on her rosy face.

She cried, "Dad! Jill!"

In the kitchen, Jared kneed Cody's crotch. Cody felt like his intestines tightened around each other, tied together like shoelaces on a sneaker. He opened his mouth and gasped for air, releasing Jared's throat in the process. Jared gave him a bear hug, wrapping his arms around his waist. He lifted him from the floor, then he slammed him on the kitchen island. Pots and pans rained down on them from the rack above the island.

Jared grabbed the sides of Cody's head. He lifted his head, then he slammed the back of his head against the counter. Cody's skull emitted a loud *thud* and a *crunch.* Blood drizzled out of his scalp. His eyes rolled back, he coughed, and then he vomited. The brown puke landed on his bruises, bloody face. He lost control of his body, so he couldn't fight back. Jared slammed his head on the countertop again—*and again.*

He yelled, "Look what you made me do! I could have gotten away! You fucking idiot!"

Jared slid on the floor as he turned to leave. He looked back at Cody's face, then at the teenager's hand. Cody, eyes half-open, held onto the bottom of Jared's jacket. His arms and wrists were broken with a baseball bat, he suffered from a concussion and brain damage due to the blows he took to the head, but his grip was strong. Something inside of him told him to fight for the Cohen family. *Buy a little more time,* the little voice in his head said, *make things right, stop him and save them.*

Jared swung down at him with a barrage of jabs. He yelled, "Let! Me! *Go!*"

The windows and lightbulbs exploded in the kitchen and living room. The ceiling groaned as it fought the heat.

"Cody, stop!" Jared shouted. "You fucking asshole!"

Jared grabbed the chest of Cody's hoodie with both hands, then he slid him off the kitchen island. Cody hit the floor head-first. He convulsed due to the severe head trauma. His limbs tightened up. He clenched his fists and gritted his teeth. Blood and saliva foamed out of his mouth. Yet, Jared couldn't pry Cody's hand open to free himself. He opened the oven and pushed Cody's head inside. He slammed the door on his head.

One time, two times, three times.

A gash opened up Cody's right temple. His skull was visible through his wet hair and the gushing blood. His right eye hemorrhaged.

Four times, five times, six times.

The cut widened and stretched, reaching from his eyebrow to his ear. The left side of his face was bruised. His right eye, slimy blood oozing out of it, popped out of his eye socket.

Seven times, eight times.

With the seventh blow, Cody released his grip on Jared's jacket. His limp arms fell to the floor. If Jared weren't holding his hoodie, he would have fallen to the floor, too. His skull was broken. A shard of his bone stabbed his brain. Blood raced down every crevice of his brain, like a massive wave flowing through water canals in a city. His skull was flooded with blood. He passed away.

With the eighth blow, his skull collapsed in on itself. Part of his eye hung over his cheekbone while the rest was crushed in the caved in socket. One of the oven door's hinges broke. The edge of the door screeched on the marble floor. Jared released Cody's hoodie. The young teenager hit the floor face-first. He didn't move, but Jared needed to guarantee his death.

He groaned in pain as he lifted his knee up to his stabbed stomach, then he stomped on the back of Cody's neck. Cody's spine snapped instantly, and an indentation of Jared's boot was pushed into his neck—*a crater*. His head rolled to the side with more goops of blood foaming out of his mouth. He was unrecognizable due to all of his grotesque injuries. And he wasn't going to stand up and interfere again.

Jared stumbled through the kitchen, coughing and wheezing. The smoke obscured his vision. He saw orange and black. He removed his jacket, then he disarmed himself so as not to get shot by the police if he were caught. He staggered, lightheaded from the brawl. He caught himself on a counter, inadvertently wetting his sleeves with some unignited gasoline.

"Shit," he muttered as he shook his head wildly. "Focus, Jared. You've got this."

Holding his shirt over his mouth and one hand

over his perforated stomach, he exited the kitchen through an archway. He stepped to the right, then to his left, then he spun around. The thick smoke, the unbearable heat, and the loss of blood rendered him lethargic and disoriented. The modest house felt like a mansion.

He heard shouting to his right. *Police,* he thought. He followed the voices, his head down and mouth covered as if he were walking through a sandstorm. His eyes widened as he spotted the emergency lights through the smoke. He felt the breeze, too. He crouched, lowered his shirt, and drew a deep breath. Although he inhaled some smoke, he savored the hint of fresh air. It sent a sense of relief through his body. *I'm going to make it,* he told himself, *I'm out of here.*

Before he could reach the door, Patrick lunged at him from behind. He wrapped his arm around Jared's neck and put him in a rear-naked chokehold. They fell back on the floor. Patrick landed on his back and Jared landed on top of Patrick. Jared swung his limbs and rocked from side-to-side, like a turtle stuck on his back.

He shouted, "What is wrong with you people?! Let me go, damn it!"

Patrick leaned closer to Jared's ear and said, "Fuck... you."

"You rat! You fucking rat!"

"You're not... getting away. Prison... I can't... let you live... like that. No luxury, no peace... You'll burn here... then you'll burn in Hell."

"You pussy! You're dead! Your family's dead because of you! This won't save you, you dumb-shit! You'll burn! Like your girls! Like your son!"

Jared laughed maniacally. Sweat and blood wiped the clown makeup off his face, but he sounded like a villainous clown in a horror movie. Then he was interrupted by a coughing spell. He gagged as Patrick squeezed his neck. He turned left and right, but he couldn't escape. The roar of the fire grew louder behind them. The fire spread into the bedrooms, swallowing everything in its path.

Jared was struck with something he hadn't felt since he was a child: *fear.* He lived as an outlaw—fighting, stabbing, and shooting his enemies while poisoning his community with an arsenal of addictive drugs all in the name of the Almighty Dollar—but he never truly faced his own mortality until that moment in the burning house. He didn't want to die.

He scratched Patrick's forearm, kicked at the air, and pleaded, "Please let me go! Please, man! I'm sorry! Don't let me die like this! Don't–" He coughed violently. He grimaced and cried, "I–I'm begging you! I'm so fucking sorry, man! Let me go… let me go…"

He cut into Patrick's forearm with his fingernails, tearing off chunks of skin and patches of hair with each scratch. Patrick's blood sprinkled onto Jared's face. It was hot—*boiling,* like soup in a cauldron. Patrick's head fell back and hit the floorboard. He watched the billowing cloud of smoke as it moved towards the front door. He smirked and snickered. He wanted to kill Jared, but he was satisfied by the panic in the young man's voice.

"Someone… will… get you," he whispered. "Die here… or die there. Your choice."

Patrick succumbed to his injuries. Jared pushed his arm off him. He lifted his shirt up to his mouth as he coughed again. He struggled to his feet. The smoke blinded him while the fire deafened him. He couldn't see the emergency lights or hear the voices. He teetered to his right. He crashed into one of the dining chairs.

He muttered, "No, not this way. It's over–"

As he turned around, a spark from the burning sofa landed on his long-sleeve shirt. The spark ignited the gasoline on his sleeve.

"Shit!" Jared shouted.

He staggered back as he swung his arm in every direction. The flame spread up to his shoulder, then across the back of his shirt. He tried to take it off, but it was too tight. His other sleeve was set aflame by a burning chip of wood from the ceiling. A chair fell over and then another one. His chest tightened and his lungs stung as he struggled to breathe.

He stammered, "N–N–No, p–please."

He felt another draft. He didn't think about it. He lurched towards the fresh air. Head-first, he ran through the intact patio door. He fell to the floor just three meters away from the pool. A large shard of glass protruded from his forehead. One end stuck out of his hairline while the other poked through his eyebrow. The glass cracked under his skin. Smaller shards stabbed his cheeks, nose, and neck. He was knocked senseless by the crash.

The fire spread to his jeans, burning holes into his clothes and torching his flesh. It wasn't enough to revitalize him. He felt the heat from the fire caressing the nape of his neck. Then the fire ignited the gasoline on his scalp. The sound of his hair *crackling* and the sulfuric stench of his scalp burning jolted him awake.

He gasped for air, pushed himself up to his hands and knees, and glanced around. Survival was the only thing on his mind. He scrambled towards the pool, then he jumped into the water. Smoke billowed skyward into the night sky from his body while blood billowed downward into the water from his wounds.

Panic had a way of warping a person's thoughts. It led to knee-jerk reactions—innocent fumbles, honest mistakes, *fatal miscalculations.*

Panic told Jared: *fire is bad, water is good.* It made sense to him, so he jumped into the pool. But panic failed to mention one thing: *Jared, you can't swim.*

Jared splashed and screamed, but he quickly sank. He stood on his tiptoes at the bottom of the pool. The water reached the bridge of his nose. So, he hopped in place and continued to splash. He screamed with each bounce, too, hoping someone would come to his rescue. His screaming was muffled by the sound of emergency sirens and the crepitations from the burning house.

"Pl–Please," he cried before swallowing another mouthful of water.

Slowly but surely, the water flooded his sooty, charred lungs. After a minute, he couldn't jump anymore. Floating to the surface was no longer an option, either. He tried to swim to the edge of the pool, but he could barely move. One of his lungs burst due to the excessive water and the damage caused by the fire. He grimaced in pain and gritted his teeth until his gums bled.

His skin was warm, but his abdominal cavity was cold. His throat tightened as his vocal cords spasmed and sealed off his airway. The water poured into his stomach instead. He was bloated like a balloon, but he still couldn't float to the surface. His racing heart slowed to a crawl. His vision faded as he reached for the pool's wall. His lips flapped.

He mouthed: *please.*

Then he passed away. His motionless body floated at the bottom of the pool. Police surrounded the house and watched for any survivors while firefighters fought the flames. Paramedics rushed Kimberly to the hospital. She was the sole survivor of the massacre, but *everything* was taken from her. She felt like she died that night. Hooked up to an IV, treated by a pair of gentle paramedics, she could only think about her family—Patrick, Shannon, Dustin, Jill.

Teary-eyed, fading out of consciousness, she looked at a female paramedic and asked, "Are they okay?"

Join the mailing list!

Did you enjoy this disturbing novel? Are you eager to invade another home? I'm not working on a sequel to this novel, but I frequently publish new books with similar themes. My work is dark, disgusting, and provocative. I am an author of unrelenting human horror, although I have dabbled in everything—splatterpunk, supernatural, psychological, fantasy, science-fiction, and more. And best of all, I release *at least* eight books a year!

By signing up for my mailing list, you'll be the first to know about my newest books, my massive book sales, and other important news. You may even get the chance to listen to one of my audiobooks before everyone else! You'll usually receive one email per month. You *might* receive two or three during some busier months, and you might receive none during slower months. Either way, you have my word: I will *never* spam you. The process is fast, easy, and free, so visit this link to sign-up: http://eepurl.com/bNl1CP.

Dear Reader,

Thank you for reading *Trespassers.* This was a very bleak and depressing project for me, so I'm glad you stuck to it until the end. I'm glad I'm not alone and *someone* is reading this letter. I'll get down to all of the juicy behind-the-scene details soon, but, first—being the gentleman I am—I have to apologize to those who may have been offended by the contents of this book. I mean it this time. *Really!* There were some truly disturbing sequences in this book, some of which involved children/teenagers. But, like I always say, just remember: *it's only a book.*

'It's only a book.'

In this case, I find this statement a bit humorous. This book is a work of fiction. That is true. However, this book was also inspired by *real* events. The basis of this novel was inspired by the tragic Cheshire, Connecticut home invasion murders where two ~~men~~ pieces of shit robbed, tortured, and murdered an innocent family. I had been planning on writing a *The Strangers/The Purge*-inspired novel since the end of last year. So, as usual, I spent months studying *real* invasions and watching films in the subgenre. This case changed *everything.* The story I had planned went from a fast-paced, gory slasher with a high kill count to a bleak, nihilistic, and violent story of despair.

Of course, when it comes to these types of things, I never want to be disrespectful to the victims of real crimes and I don't want to glorify real criminals, so I made many significant changes. The cast of characters, the setting, and the motives are all different, for example. From the drug-addicted trespassers to the quiet Cohen family, the Halloween backdrop to the Nevada setting, almost everything is different. I think of this novel as a reflection of reality—an *honest* reflection of what people do to each other in the real world. Anyway, I suppose the inspiration behind this book is the reason why it felt so raw and depressing to me. Maybe you'll feel the same now.

Remember, monsters like Jared and desperate people like Crystal and Cody exist in our world. And *anyone* can be a victim, including you and me. And, as an additional note, if you believe the police response in this book was unrealistic, check out the response to the Cheshire, Connecticut case as well as other similar home invasion cases. Sometimes, the police response can be tragically slow and ineffective.

The book was also inspired and even modeled after some classic home invasion films, such as *Straw Dogs, The Last House on the Left* (including the impressive remake), and *I Spit on Your Grave.* Now, not all of these are home invasion movies in the strictest definition of the subgenre, but they share similar themes and settings. I was also inspired by Jack Ketchum, my favorite author if you haven't noticed by now, and Dean Koontz's *Intensity*. I really should have read more home invasion novels to prepare for this project, but I couldn't find many. If you have any recommendations (including books you might have written yourself), send them over to my email, which you'll find at the end of this letter.

But, *before* you do that, maybe you can stop by Amazon.com (or your local Amazon store if you're one of my international readers!) and leave a review. You can also leave a review on Goodreads, Bookbub, your blog, or even post a quick one on Twitter. It all helps! Your feedback helps me improve and it helps me choose my next project. Your reviews also help other readers find this book, which leads to *more* books in the future. I always say this because it's true: your reviews and your messages keep me motivated. You already took several hours of your day to read through this book, so I really appreciate it when you take a few more minutes to write a review or send me a message.

If you need help writing your review, you can try answering questions like these: did you enjoy the story? Was it too disturbing, just right, or not violent enough for an extreme horror book? Were you satisfied with the ending? Would you like to read more stories inspired by true crimes in the future? Your review can be long and detailed or short and direct. It's very helpful either way.

I'm writing this letter on August 13, 2019. I am sitting on the floor in a tiny apartment in Tokyo, Japan, typing away at my laptop while I try not to nod off after finishing another eight-hour writing/editing session fueled by ramen and Red Bull. And I'm *very* happy right now. (It feels a little weird typing that out after I just explained how this project left me emotionally drained, but I can't really pretend like I'm not happy.) I'm glad to have the opportunity to be here again. It's a wonderful place for inspiration and, since I don't have stable wi-fi this time around, it's a great place to get some writing done without any distractions... unless I go outside. As usual, I have to thank *you* for helping me get this far in my career. As cliché as it may sound, I'm nothing without you. So, I hope I can deliver a very special book to you in November or December. It's something that a lot of people have been asking for. I'm calling it *A Fistful of Guts* and it's the sequel to *The Good, the Bad, and the Sadistic.* I can't wait to share more with you soon!

If you enjoyed this book, please visit my Amazon's author page and check out my other novels. As I've mentioned before, I release new books frequently—eight to twelve a year, although I've slowed down a bit recently. I am an extreme horror author who focuses on 'human horror,' which I like to think of as a hybrid of true crime and splatter horror. It's about real people doing awful things to other real people. It's about things that can happen to me or *you*. I also write in other genres/subgenres. I release a new supernatural horror book every year or so. My last book, *Maneater,* was about a woman who stalks and torments her ex-boyfriend. My next book, *A Fistful of Guts,* is a sequel to *The Good, the Bad, and the Sadistic.* Homicide Detective Harvey Skinner continues his secret program, allowing Sam Lee—known as *The Heartless Heart-Ripper*—to hunt suspected serial killers across the country. I hope you'll enjoy these new projects. Once again, thank you for reading!

Until our next venture into the dark and disturbing,
Jon Athan

P.S. If you have any questions or comments, or if you're an aspiring author who needs *some* help, feel free to contact me directly using my business email: info@jon-athan.com. You can also contact me through Twitter @Jonny_Athan or my Facebook page.

Made in the USA
Columbia, SC
27 October 2022